PAINT AND PENALTIES

Rochester Copperheads

Book 1

RJ SCOTT

V.L. LOCEY

Love Lane Books

Copyright

A note to readers

Paint & Penalties was first released in October 2025 as part of *The Games We Play – Season 2* shared world, under the original title *Rough Draft*. You can still check out the rest of Season 2 here from lots of different authors!

We loved this world — and especially the Rochester Copperheads — so much that it grew into an entire new series of its own.

The next book in this series, *Spectrum & Smoke*, releases in just a few days and is available now for preorder on Amazon & Kindle Unlimited, with more books in the series coming soon!

With love, RJ & Vicki

ROCHESTER COPPERHEADS

1. *Paint & Penalties* (formerly *Rough Draft*)
2. *Spectrum & Smoke*
3. *Grief & Glitter*
4. *Frost & Firelight*

Paint and Penalties

He was supposed to be the NHL's next superstar. Now Walker Hannan is one penalty, one bad decision, and one final chance away from losing everything.

Banished to the minors after becoming the kind of player coaches warn rookies about, Walker's only focus is clawing his way back to the NHL before his career crashes for good. Then Finn Carter—an annoyingly optimistic art teacher with paint-stained hands and zero interest in Walker's reputation—walks into his life and turns everything upside down.

What starts as an impossible attraction turns into something neither of them expected: late nights, stolen kisses, found family, and the terrifying possibility of something real.

But just when Walker starts wanting more than hockey, the NHL comes calling with the second chance he's been waiting for.

Now he has to decide what matters more—the career he's fought for his entire life, or the man teaching him there's life beyond the ice.

Paint and Penalties is a grumpy/sunshine, opposites attract MM hockey romance packed with emotional hurt/comfort, found family, redemption, chemistry, and a hard-won HEA.

*****

Content warning: This story has references to substance abuse, self-harm, childhood violence, school shooting, off-page physical child abuse, and mental health concerns.

Dedication

To my family who accepts me and all my foibles and quirks. Even the plastic banana in my holster.
VL Locey

Always for my family.
RJ Scott

PAINT & *Penalties*

RJ SCOTT & V.L. LOCEY

ONE

Walker

NOT GOING TO LIE, THERE WAS SOMETHING ABOUT A night on the dance floor.

Maybe it was the pulsing lights. Maybe it was the thumping beat of a Gucci Mayne song playing so loudly it made your ears weep. Maybe it was the crush of bodies packed tightly together, with the smell of aftershave, perfume, sweat, and sex. Maybe it was all of the above. Probably so. Whatever the reason, I was shoulder deep in sexy men of all shapes, colors, and personalities. Bears, twinks, daddies, and gym bunnies. You name it, and you could find it at Arrows Down, the premier gay club in Soho.

Massive dance floor, basement stage for drag shows, and an open-air piano bar on the roof for the queers who wanted something a little less in their face. A dude in a shiny pink dress with long blond hair shimmied up to me, wiggling between the two bears who had decided they wanted a jock filler for their hairy sandwich. Something I was totally down for because, hey, a guy only lives once. I was twenty-five, playing hockey for the New York Vipers, and hauling in a cool couple million per year. Why not enjoy the gifts that the hockey gods had blessed me with?

"Do I know you?" Slinky Pink Dress asked as he rubbed his slim form against me. I twisted from the two bears to smile at Goldilocks. "You look so familiar."

"Maybe," I shouted to be heard over Gucci, slapping my hands on his thin hips, then pulling him to my thigh. He began to roll his hips, his glimmery dress riding high on his bare leg. A smooth leg. Yum. Just my type. Lean, pretty, and horny. "I play hockey."

"Oh no, that's not it. You do a commercial for that car dealership in Hoboken." He ran his fingers over my chest, manicured pink nails finding my nipples through my shirt. I twitched, and so did my dick. "You're so sexy in that commercial. Want to come to my place and see what I have under my hood?"

I laughed out loud. Probably too loud, but I was

nicely buzzed. "I can feel what you have under the hood, Goldilocks."

He giggled. I was hooked instantly. I turned to the two burly bears and shrugged as Goldi led me out of the club into a cool New York night. The city beat thrummed through the sidewalk as we stumbled along, touching and laughing at passersby. A few people turned to gape. I was used to that. The Vipers were *the* New York team. And we all knew that if you made it in the Big Apple, you'd made it. And I had fucking made it. Walker Hannan was pretty big shit. And rightfully so. I'd suffered countless heartaches for this fucking sport. It was time for it to pay me back as I deserved. With cash, hot guys, and plenty of fan adoration.

I had a belly full of top-shelf whiskey mixed with poppers. Nothing big, just a couple to get the night rocking.

I pinned Goldi against the brick wall of a Korean market. We made out for several minutes until someone walking past yelled at us to get a room.

Bouncing off the walls and each other, we fumbled along, Goldi wobbling badly on his stilettos, until we rounded a corner. Outside a small movie theater was a dude dressed up like some sort of squid. It freaked me out for a second before I realized it was a guy in a suit and not a giant squid on the corner of Wooster and Prince. I chuckled at my stupidity as I grasped a streetlight to help level out the wavy street.

"Oh look, it's a squid!" Goldi squealed. "Now stand there with him. Give me your phone so I can take your picture."

Being a moron who had a soft spot for men with big eyes and soft mouths—and also slightly inebriated and a wee bit high—I did as Goldi asked and tossed him my phone.

He smiled so cutely I was momentarily stunned. The guy in the squid suit muttered something in a very Bronx accent before stuffing a ticket for a buck off a large drink into my hand. I asked the squid what the movie was about. He said a squid. I turned to smile for the camera only to see Goldi streaking down the sidewalk.

"Motherfucker!" I snarled, tossed the big squid aside, and set off after my phone. It was a month old, and yeah, it held all kinds of things that were personal. It was a no-contest sprint. Goldi in high heels versus a hockey player who creamed everyone on his team during off-ice speed sprints. I dove at Goldi. He hit the pavement hard, crying out as his knees and chin scraped along the sidewalk. People jumped back, shouted, and started taking video as I rolled Goldi over, took my fucking phone, and then punched him a few times in the face. His nose crunched, his wig fell off, and four guys yanked me off the weeping thief. They probably thought I was assaulting a woman, but to their credit, when his wig came off, they still wrestled me away, so good on them for looking out for the femme dudes in New York City.

It took all four men to keep me held to the wall until the cops arrived. Goldi was taken to the hospital, and I was taken into custody.

Things went sort of downhill after that, but I had my phone. No one steals shit from Walker Hannan.

No. One.

MY SISTER POSTED MY BAIL.

My agent called me to bail.

And now, a day later, sitting in the posh office of the New York Vipers' general manager, I was pretty sure the team was going to bail as well.

Life sure can be a bitch.

"Walker, we need to do something about your situation," Mike said as he studied me over the top of some thick-ass glasses. Mike Gallows was an old-timer. He had played for Boston back in the day -- tough as nails, always finished his checks, and skated with an edge. Like me, only now that he was wearing a suit and tie and not skates, his attitude about that edge had shifted significantly. Along with most of the league. "This is your fourth problematic encounter with the police during your year and a half with the team. You were publicly intoxicated and have assault charges filed against you by the young man you beat up."

"Two punches, Mike, maybe three. That's hardly what I would call a beatdown."

He took a moment to close his dark eyes, then reopened them to pin me to the wall like a fly.

"The young man is five-four and weighs a hundred twenty pounds. You're six-four and weigh two-ten."

"He stole my phone, Mike."

"Okay, you are going to have to start addressing me as Mr. Gallows. I've done all I can to keep you on this team because you're an asset on the ice. Off the ice, you're a fucking liability. So, to that end, the Vipers are *strongly* advising you to enter the abuse and behavior program to get your addictions under control."

"Mike." His frown deepened. "Mr. Gallows. I do

not have an addiction problem. I was drunk. Sure. We had just won a big game. I went out to celebrate. Maybe I did overindulge, but one night on the town does not an addiction problem make."

A vein in his cheek twitched. "As I said, you should strongly consider signing into a rehab program for at least thirty days. If you do not wish to avail yourself of the league's program, which is quite good, I understand, you may choose a program that suits you better. After you are released, you will report to the Rochester Copperheads."

My jaw dropped. "You're sending me down for one little altercation?"

"Walker, this is four." He held up four scarred fingers. A lifetime of fights and slashes could be seen on those meaty digits. "Four altercations that involved the police." I was going to argue. I was good at that, but when I saw the resignation on his face, I flopped back into the nicely padded chair I was sitting in and crossed my arms over my nice blue suit jacket. "So, once you have completed your time with a counselor for anger and substance issues, you will report to the Copperheads. There, you will work on your game while attending weekly counseling sessions with a team-appointed anger management counselor. Then, we'll look at your progress and stats at the end of the season to see if you're ready to return to the Vipers."

"That sucks."

"No, this team is bending over backward to help you help yourself. I know you had a problematic childhood. I also like you. I like how hardnosed you are, how you hit the ice with passion and grit, and how you can shoot the puck. So, to that end, go get your head pulled out of your ass, help out the Copperheads, and try to find something in your life that'll make you happy."

"Hockey makes me happy." I sounded like a truculent child, but it was the truth. There was little else that did, other than my sister Harper, but even she was weary of my shit and had told me so at full volume while driving me home from the first precinct.

Mike nodded sadly. "I know it does, but, son, there is a lot more to life than hockey. Try to find some balance. Hell, learn to meditate or do some yoga. Sip some green tea chai shit. Write poetry. Go for walks in nature. Journal. Find out what the kids are doing today to reach that happy hippy state and do that. Whatever brings you some damn happiness outside of the rink."

"Mike, this sucks. We've only played ten games.

The Vipers need me." My arguments were weak. I knew it, but fuck, I had to try.

"I know, Walker. We'll manage. Go fix yourself. We'll talk next summer."

That dismissal was as blunt as the crooked nose on Mike's face. What could I do but rise, shake his hand, and slink out of the office like a whipped mutt? Nothing.

I made my way to the end of the corridor to look down at the fresh ice so far below. The team logo at center ice taunted me as I dashed at the sudden dampness on my face. My father's voice hit me like a crosscheck to the kidneys. It had been years since his death, but his words lived on forever inside my head.

What the hell are you crying for? Men don't cry. Now get up off the ice and come at me again, and this time, don't hit like a girl.

Hockey players didn't cry either. They hit things. Hard. Repeatedly. And without empathy.

"Fuck you tons, Dad," I murmured to the rink, the only place where I'd once felt some peace, and drove a fist into the thick wall of plexiglass before entering the elevator. The ache in my knuckles matched the pain in my breast, but I swallowed it down like a loose chiclet.

Men didn't cry. Men dealt. Men grew a pair.

Since I already had a pretty big set of balls, I guess I would have to find another way to express my emotions without sniffles or snivels. Or fists.

If they made me paint with oils in rehab, I would not be happy at all. Not all of us wanted to be Bob "I am so soothing people watch me to drift off to sleepy land" Ross. Soft guys didn't finish first.

We all knew that.

TWO

Finn

I STUDIED THE PAINTING CAREFULLY, DRAWN IN BY the bold colors and the passion radiating from each layer of thick paint. Something about it struck a chord in me as if the artist had thrown every emotion they had onto the canvas, hoping something would stick. The texture felt almost violent, yet there was a fragile vulnerability in how the colors clashed but somehow worked together. The strokes were heavy, rough enough to nearly tear through the canvas. It was as if the brush had been wielded with raw emotion, desperate to make a point. A potent mix of chaos and intention I couldn't stop staring at.

"Wow," I said.

It was a house with an orange roof that slanted steeply like a witch's hat. The perspective skewed and impossibly challenging. The sun in the corner looked furious, all jagged lines and angry yellow swirls. A family was scattered in front of the house, and I loved the boldness and confidence in each imperfect line. There was no hesitation, no second-guessing, just raw, unapologetic creativity, the kind I wished I could channel before self-doubt crushed me. I loved the passion, the energy, and the way the colors seemed to pulse with life—just as captivating as any old master. It reminded me of Van Gogh's wild brushwork or the emotional intensity of a Munch painting. Art that didn't just depict a scene but made you feel it. That was what this piece did. It grabbed me by the collar and refused to let go.

"And that's Muppet, my cat," a paint-crusted finger pointed at a dark blob, which channeled Jackson Pollock.

"Wow," I repeated, pouring as much genuine awe into my voice as I could manage, my enthusiasm never faltering.

"Is it okay?"

I lifted my gaze and met Jamie's wide eyes as he awaited my opinion. His fingers were twisted in his purple shirt, and his expression was uncertain.

He'd been quiet all day, which wasn't like him. Sweet and angelic by name but a holy terror in every other way, the six-year-old would shove the paper in my face and demand I tell him he was brilliant. I made a mental note that the male figure in the painting—dad, I assumed—was standing some distance from the mom and the two kids, plus, of course, Muppet, the cat. Placing the dad apart like that could mean so many things. Maybe Jamie had overheard an argument or the dad had taken away a toy or perhaps it was something bigger, like a family breakup. I'd mention it at the end-of-day briefing to see if anyone knew anything because it might explain why Jamie had seemed off today.

One of the things I'd learned over the years was how much a child's home life could appear in their drawings. A house set apart, a family member drawn smaller or further away. Sometimes those little details told stories kids didn't know how to put into words. It wasn't always a sign of trouble, but I'd seen enough to know when something felt off.

Anyway, back to the art side of teaching a class of first-grade students.

"I'm going to pin it to the amazing wall of awesome," I declared, and he beamed at me. Little did the class realize, but everyone got their chance on that wall on rotation—no child left behind—and when they did make it up there, they lit up like fireworks.

Every piece my students created was amazing, even the sheets with just a splash of color in the center reflected their world, feelings, and imagination.

Jamie bolted back to his table, shouting to his best friend, "I told you he'd love it!" Now, there was the happy, smiling Jamie I knew.

I grinned and shook my head, turning my attention back to the classroom. Twenty kids spread across mismatched tables, with pencils and crayons scattered like confetti. The air buzzed with chatter, laughter, and the occasional shriek. Some kids were deep in concentration, tongues poking from the corners of their mouths as they furiously shaded in rainbows or crafted stick-figure masterpieces. Others shared crayons like traders at a bustling market, bartering for the best shades of red or blue. This end-of-day art session was chaotic, but it was also full of life. The kind of energy that made teaching feel less like a job and more like a privilege.

I made my way around the tables, offering help, praising color, breaking up a small fight over the last purple crayon, and frowning at the stain in the corner that had expanded since last night's rain. Gladwell Elementary, Rochester, was a tired old thing—all peeling paint and drafty windows—but I loved it here. This was my third year of teaching, and I still felt lucky every day to walk into this room and see those eager faces. I just wished there was a budget for remedial work to fix the wall. Maybe I'd grab Connor over the weekend, and between us, we could paint over the stain as a shortstop and, perhaps, even figure out where the rain was coming in. My big sports-playing brother might be an idiot at times, and the bane of my life, but he loved his DIY.

Teaching these kids was everything. If it meant less time for my art, that was life. It was a work in progress. My parents had panicked when I mentioned being a full-time artist. "There's no money in art," they'd said in unison. I was a good son who listened to his mom and dad, and compromised his fine art dreams, choosing a career in early childhood education, teaching for stability while creating art in quiet moments. Weekends were for painting, and evenings were for class prep. And my volunteer work —running art therapy sessions at the local community center and sometimes the hospital—was my way of keeping my passion alive.

Lessons complete, materials put away, one by one, parents whisked away my six-year-olds to their homes. I tried to catch Jamie's mom's eye, but she'd always been a run-and-no-stopping kind of mom, so I didn't get a chance to talk.

The classroom fell into a rare silence. I padded around fixing things, putting the room to rights by straightening the paintings on the wall, wiping down a few desks, and gathering stray crayons that'd rolled under tables. The quiet was oddly soothing, the calm after the storm of twenty energetic kids buzzing through my space.

Emma, a fellow teacher and friend, appeared in the doorway. She looked exhausted, her face pale with that familiar glassy-eyed expression I'd seen a hundred times before.

"I've got it," she said dramatically.

I knew exactly what she meant. A cold. The one that bounced permanently between kids and teachers, no matter how hard we tried to dodge it. It was as inevitable as sticky fingers on freshly cleaned windows or someone spilling juice five minutes after lunch started.

I skirted her to get out of the classroom, crossing my fingers in front of me. "No, I don't want it again!"

"Too late!" she rasped in her best zombie voice, arms outstretched as she staggered after me. I laughed, dodging her grasp as we made our way down the corridor. Kids' coats still dangled from hooks, and an abandoned backpack slumped by the water fountain. The school felt quieter, almost peaceful, but Emma's dramatic performance kept the mood light.

We reached the hall for the post-day meet up. Our principal, Tonya Lewis, was a stickler for communication, a fact I appreciated more than I could say. Clear communication kept everything running smoothly, which was no small thing in a job that constantly balanced chaos and calm.

There were ten of us at Gladwell, ten teachers— nine women and me—and we stood in a loose circle, all giving Emma a wide berth. Conversation buzzed around us, snippets of lesson anecdotes, laughter, and plans for the weekend. Emma kept sniffling theatrically, wiping her nose with an ever-dwindling tissue supply. When it was my turn to talk, I mentioned Jamie and the painting. I kept my tone casual, but I described the details: how his dad had been set apart in the picture, how Jamie had seemed off today, and there'd been moments of stress over the last couple of weeks. "He gets in fights with some of the others, but y'know it always blows over, and he's back to happy-Jamie. Might be nothing... but I thought I'd flag it just in case," I added.

The meeting was done, and I headed for the car. I loved my job, but there was something about Fridays that just made everything feel lighter. That sense of release after a long week, knowing I didn't have to prep lessons or break up fights over crayons for two whole days, was like a breath of fresh air.

Tonight, though, I wasn't heading straight home. I had a brand-new art class lined up. Confidential. I didn't have many details, but the man who booked me had assured me it was a small group of five, and I'd have access to whatever supplies I needed.

The NDA had been unexpected and unusual for a simple art class, but it only made things more intriguing. Maybe it was for a prominent Hollywood actor, a politician, or a millionaire businessman. Who knew? The mystery added to the excitement building in my chest as I drove away from the school. The thought of fresh paint and eager people wanting to learn all the mysteries of art filled my mind.

I arrived at the address, a modern community center in an affluent neighborhood, with floor-to-ceiling windows and fresh landscaping that still smelled faintly of mulch. The parking lot was lined with high-end cars. Sleek BMWs, a polished Mercedes SUV, and a striking red Audi that looked like it had never seen a muddy road. Even the less flashy vehicles had a certain gloss to them, the kind of cars that belonged to people who had them detailed every other week. If the cars were any indication, people with money were here. I patted the dashboard fondly when I parked my fifteen-year-old Honda Civic with its faded blue paint. "Don't worry," I murmured. "I still love you."

Flustered and breathless, a young woman was waiting inside the door, her clipboard clutched tightly to her chest as if it might escape if she let go. Her hair, twisted into a messy bun, had strands rebelling in all directions, and her glasses perched crookedly on her nose. She looked like she'd just finished wrangling a herd of stampeding children or perhaps something wilder. "Mr. Carter?" she asked, her voice hopeful yet strained. I fished out my school ID and held it up. Relief instantly softened her face. "Oh, thank God," she breathed, then jabbed her finger down a corridor. "Room seven. Good luck."

I wanted to ask her what she meant, but she launched out the door and scurried away as fast as her Louboutins would let her. Only her words lingered, carrying just enough weight to make me pause. Not ominous exactly, but enough to make me wonder what I'd walked into.

Okay, what could be worse than a room full of six-year-olds?

I stopped at the door, took a deep breath, and squared my shoulders. My rucksack of supplies dug into my back, so I adjusted the straps. Then, conjuring up my best "I'm ready for anything" smile, I grasped the door handle, steeling myself for whatever lay beyond, and walked in.

The room was in chaos. Five big men—broad-shouldered, muscled, and towering—filled the space. Each wore some variation of sweatpants and jerseys, but nothing was relaxed about the tension crackling in the air.

Two of them were locked in a struggle, shoving and swearing, their voices rough and sharp. The scrape of shoes against the floor was loud, and a chair skidded sideways with a loud clatter as one man shoved the other back. They were shouting and cursing—I think one of them in French—filling the room with a tension that made my skin prickle. One furious man had another pinned against the wall, his arm pressed hard against the other's chest. Two others tried breaking it up, pulling at the angry guy and speaking urgently.

Near the back, a fifth man leaned against the wall, arms crossed, seemingly unbothered by the bedlam unfolding around him. His expression was impassive as though this was just another Friday.

I stood frozen in the doorway, my rucksack still slung over one shoulder, mouth slightly open in shock. This was definitely not what I'd expected from an art class.

"Coach!" the lounging man shouted, and the tension shifted instantly. The fight snapped apart, the angry one shoving his opponent away, sending him sprawling to the floor in a furious, sputtering crouch. The tension in the air didn't disappear, though. It just crackled, shifting focus.

The angry guy turned, and his gaze locked onto me. He had blood on his face, a thin trail seeping from a cut above his eyebrow, and his expression was murderous.

I flicked my gaze around the room, taking in the mess of overturned chairs, scattered sketchpads, and the jagged tear in one of the canvas boards. Then, my eyes landed on the sign tacked to the side wall:

Hockey Player Assistance Program—Art Class, 1/10.

My stomach turned. Jocks.

Mr. Angry was smirking now, a slow, deliberate smile that spread across his face as a wolf sighting easy prey. He stalked across the room toward me, each step heavy and intentional. Three of the other four men fell in behind him, moving as a unit, like soldiers closing ranks, but the man who'd been leaning on the wall pushed his way in front of them, and he was the one I was now facing -- brilliant brown eyes and the build of a linebacker -- and I froze. My rucksack seemed to gain weight on my shoulder, straps digging into my skin. My inner bullied child—the one who always found safety in art, the one who'd mastered the art of walking with his head down, slipping through school corridors unnoticed, and escaping into sketchbooks filled with worlds no one could touch—curled up and died on the spot. Memories flickered back. Sharp whispers, locker slams, and laughter that always seemed to follow me home. Those feelings prickled under my skin, my breath catching in my throat as five towering figures closed in.

This was way worse than a class of six-year-olds.

THREE

Walker

THE MAN WHO I ASSUMED WAS THE ART TEACHER looked as if he'd just walked into the lion's den clad in only a breechcloth with a slingshot in his hand. Then, because the little man with the soulful hazel eyes hadn't pinged my radar enough simply by being slim, blondish, and adorable, he jerked up his chin. Ah. So, we had David facing down five Goliaths. Dad's Bible readings in the evenings had paid off, it seemed. Lucky me and Harper. Beatings at six, biblical hour at seven, bed by eight. Hallelujah. No rod was spared in our home.

I felt the slight surge of upset that thinking about my father always brought, but it was dulled. Go mood stabilizers. Pity the other side effects weren't as enjoyable as my head and body adjusted to the newest prescription. The headaches and lethargy were shitty, which meant I wasn't allowed to drive or play hockey. Not even for the Copperheads. Nothing that could be considered dangerous for another two months. That gets us well into January. Half the season gone, and here I was sitting in Rochester with no wheels, no hockey, but tons of fucking therapy programs. Talk, talk, talk. That was all I did on the daily. Rehash old trauma, skate at the Copperheads rink, and go to my new apartment to dwell. Thank God Harper had come with me on this temporary move, or I would have thrown myself off the balcony of my condo that overlooked Lake Ontario. Kidding. Mostly.

"I'm not the coach. I'm your teacher. You all may call me Mr. Carter. Now, please tidy up this mess and place your canvases back on your easels."

Mr. Cuteness spoke up in a teacher voice that stalled all the other orangutans in this mandated art class. All five of us were Copperheads. And all five were here for various reasons, which the other guys had not divulged, aside from Bob, who talked all the time. Totally fair. I'd not told them my issues other than what they could read about in the press.

"Okay, apes, you heard the man. Tell him your names and then tidy up. It's time to fingerpaint," I barked to the four hulks. "I'm Walker." Mr. Carter gave me a curt nod as the other bozos called out their first names. He then gave me an appreciative look before spinning to march to the old metal desk at the front of the room to drop his satchel. He had a nice ass. Tiny but firm. Each little cheek a handful. When he stopped at the desk, the setting sun touched his hair to bring out soft red highlights in the dirty blond mass.

"Mais bien sûr," Arnaud replied. The lanky French-Canadian second-string goalie gave the teacher a wide and very charming smile before nudging the other chuckleheads into doing as directed. For some bizarre reason, the four seemed to follow orders from me rather well. Maybe I just had that kind of tone, or perhaps they were lost like me and desperate for someone to lead them along the straight and narrow path to recovery. If it was the second reason, the poor bastards had joined the wrong fucking wagon train. If they thought I was some wagon master, they'd be dead before we reached the border. We would ride into the lake before we even had the chance to croak from dysentery. Nope. I was not a leader.

Sensing I was supposed to be helping and not gawking at the teacher, I joined in, righted my easel, and placed the blank canvas on it.

"Wonderful. Well done. Now, I brought some paints with me and a few palettes." Mr. Carter moved through the small circle we'd made to hand out supplies. His speaking voice was calm, kind, perfect for this little group of knot heads. He had a vibe that resonated with me. Seeped into my skin to settle under the flesh to lessen the tension in me. I had found out, through thirty days of rehab, that I was more than a little tense. I was a lot tense, all the time. A duress symptom, one of the counselors had called it. Kind of like PTSD from being on the edge all the time as a kid. You never knew where the fist or kick would come from, so you lived your life stretched tight as a bowstring at full pull, ready to fire at the slightest hint of abuse.

"What are we painting?" Bob O'Ryan called from the back, his voice loud enough to cut through both the music and the hum of the heater.

Bob was a D-man. Big, burly, built like he could take a hit from a truck and barely flinch. He had a voice like gravel and hands that looked too clumsy to hold a brush, let alone do anything delicate with it. He wasn't the type anyone expected to show up for team art therapy, and from the way he slouched in his chair, arms crossed like he'd rather be anywhere else, he wasn't thrilled to be here.

His anger issues were legendary—short fuse, big reaction, worse than mine even—and they only seemed to get worse whenever Arnaud was in the room. No one ever said why. No one really had to. You could feel it in the way Bob's jaw clenched when Arnaud spoke, and how he bristled if they were paired for drills.

Now, Bob was eyeing the blank canvas like it had personally insulted him. The brush Mr. Carter handed him looked absurd in his fist.

"What are we painting?" he repeated, sharper this time.

Arnaud didn't even look up from his palette. He was already swirling red and blue together with a kind of lazy precision, like he was born holding a brush. "Your feelings, non?" he said, voice smooth, that faint French-Canadian lilt curling around the edges of his words. "But maybe for you, Bob, just painting something that isn't being an asshole would be a good start."

Bob's chair creaked as he sat forward, his knuckles tightening around the brush as if it might suddenly become a weapon. His shoulders rose, a slow, deliberate movement. It was like watching storm clouds gather.

"Say that again," he muttered. Fuck, the two

assholes were at it again. Wasn't it enough he'd already pinned Arnaud to the wall for dissing Oreos? I mean, even I'm not that bad.

Arnaud finally glanced up, eyes gleaming with amusement. "You heard me. Or do I need to speak slower for you, mon grand?"

Everyone else had gone quiet. Even Mr. Carter had stopped mid-step, holding a tray of paint like it might break the silence instead of the mood.

Bob didn't move, not really, but his jaw locked and his breathing shifted, becoming tight and shallow. He looked as if he was two seconds away from snapping the brush clean in half.

Then, from across the room, Chip piped up, not even looking up from the weird little sketch he was working on.

"Did you know that red paint increases aggressive behavior in group settings by 12.4 percent? It's something about how the brain processes warm colors under stress."

Everyone turned to look at him.

Chip finally glanced up, blinking. "What? It's a real study."

For a second, no one spoke—complete silence—until Bob let out a low grunt that could've been a laugh or just air escaping a balloon.

Arnaud smirked and went back to mixing paint, clearly pleased with himself. Mr. Carter visibly exhaled and continued passing out supplies.

"Paint what you want," Mr. Carter said as he passed out extra colors, his phone playing some soft indie thing in the background. The room smelled of stale paper and radiator heat. Classic November in Rochester, all windows sealed tight, the heater wheezing like it hated its job.

"I think we should try expressing what we're feeling in our artwork," Carter went on. "Use the primary colors on your palette to show the world where you are mentally right now."

"I don't know," Chip muttered, barely loud enough to hear. "I don't know. I don't know."

Russell "Chip" Cornish was a weird one. Not weird in a bad way, just different. He always had a stat to share, some obscure fact he'd drop into conversation like it was normal to know how many defensemen in the big leagues were called Walker, one, other than me, or which plant was poisonous and undetectable to taste. He had this little tic where he pressed his fingertips together constantly, as though he was counting something invisible. And he never quite looked me in the eye.

But damn, he was hot on the ice. His angles were

always perfect. Tight turns, smooth transitions, and never in the wrong place. It was as if his brain was wired for geometry that the rest of us couldn't see.

Right now, he was staring at what he'd started, and he was doing that finger thing again. "It's all wrong," he said. "My paper has a crease." He pointed to it, and Mr. Carter agreed there was a crease and gave him a new piece.

Meanwhile, Arnaud dipped his brush into purple paint and began creating. I glanced over at Taft, a young dude, winger, with huge green eyes and scars on his forearms. Self-harm, obviously, but that was just an educated guess. Why he'd hurt himself was his business. He was already lost in slapping color onto his canvas. Quiet sort, he kept to himself, and that was cool. Not everything in life requires a fucking dissertation.

I stared at the big white space. Mr. Carter moved around the painters, making comments, smiling softly, telling each man how good his strokes were or how expressive his color choices were. When he came to me, he gave the blank canvas a fast peek, then glanced up to find me chewing on the end of my brush.

"Painter's block?" I shrugged and chewed. "Well, sometimes it's hard to open up that locked chest of emotions and splash them all over a canvas. If you're not ready to delve that deeply, that is fine. Why don't you create a scene from something in your childhood you recall vividly?"

"Seconding that, and not sure you want to see that comment." His brown-green eyes flared, but I loaded my brush with brown and, then, made a circle. Then another one, smaller, with two pointy ears. He stood at my side, watching silently, the smell of his fruity cologne reaching my nose. I liked it. Subtle yet strong. Kind of like him. "This is Spearmint." I added some whiskers and a long cat tail to the painting. "She was our cat when my sister and I were little."

"She has lovely features," he said as I added a pair of yellow eyes. "Do you like cats?"

"Love them." I painted a pink collar with a bell. Spearmint never had a collar. She was a stray Harper and I fed on the sly. But I liked to think if things had been different, we could have brought her inside and given her a collar. "Some guys don't like cats. I think they don't because you can't force a cat to like you. Not like a dog. Cat love has to be earned. I respect that. Affection shouldn't just be handed out. A person should have to work for that privilege. When you give it to people who don't deserve it, you get kicked in the ribs."

My brush paused an inch from the canvas. Mother. Fucker. I knew it. This therapy slash meds slash mental healing was making me into Bob Ross. Next, I'd be painting happy trees and cuddling with squirrels. Not that I ever watched his show to know he sometimes had pocket squirrels or anything. I looked around to see that all four of my fellow fucked-up Copperheads were gaping at me like codfish. "What? Mind your own damn paintings." They all went back to creating masterpieces. I glanced down at Mr. Carter. He said nothing. Instead, he gave my back a soft rub as one would a child who had skinned a knee. I hated how much comfort that gave me. "I think I'm done."

"No background?" he asked, and I shook my head. "Perhaps your back yard?"

"Nope, our yard wasn't a nice place for cats," I muttered before handing my palette to the teacher, then I walked out of the classroom. I needed air. Shoving through the doors, I sucked in a lungful of cold air, let it out, and watched the tiny fog cloud float skyward before disappearing. I paced, shook out my hands, and rolled my neck. The doors opened a few minutes later, and Mr. Carter stepped out into the chilly dusk. He should have pulled on a coat. If he wanted to step closer, I could hold him to warm him up.

"Are you okay?"

I stopped circling a park bench. "Yeah, I'm good. Aces. Just needed to get out of that room. Sometimes the heat makes me congested. Stuffy nose, you know. So coming outside clears my sinuses."

"Yes, of course, that happens to all of us when the heat is turned on." He tucked his hands under his armpits. "It's going to be a fierce winter, I fear. If you'd like to come back in, we're going to clean up soon, then stroll over to the donut shop across the way for coffee and crullers."

He motioned to Mabel's Donut Shop. The shop had neon donut and coffee lights blinking in the front windows.

"No, thanks. I'm going to call my sister to come get me. Headache coming on." That part was no lie. These meds were a nightmare at times. They helped even me out, yeah, but the side effects were trash. "Meds bring them on," I tacked on when his brow furrowed in worry.

"Oh, that's a shame. Seems that way at times. Taking something to help one malady makes something else worse. Well, no worries then, Walker.

I'll clean your brushes for you this time, but next class, you will be responsible for your own tidy time."

Tidy time. Oh, holy shit. He was such a teacher. Had to be. "You teach little kids?"

"I do, yes. Oh, heck, that was a rather first-grade teacher thing to say, wasn't it?" He chuckled softly. I liked the sound of his laughter. "My apologies. Sometimes these things just slip out."

"No, hey, it's cool. I think it's nice for us, you know, a bunch of gorillas with problems."

"You're not a gorilla."

"Oh no, I meant them obviously." I threw him a wink. He smiled. "Hey, I mean, it will take my sister a long time to break free from what she's doing. I guess I could come back in to partake in tidy time, then do coffee. I don't want to be put in time-out or anything."

That bit about Harper was a total lie. I'd not even called her yet.

"Ha, ha. Very funny. I don't have a time-out chair big enough for your backside."

With that, he scooted back inside. I watched the door shut behind him, a smile playing on my lips. I liked him. He had grit. And a kindness of the soul that spoke to something buried deep inside me. Also, he was just my type. So, even though my therapist suggested not dating anyone until I had my shit straightened out -- his words, not mine, but they could have been -- I sauntered back inside the community center to find Arnaud leading the chimps in a song while they cleaned up their paints.

"Ramassez, rammasez, c'est le temps de rammasser," he croaked, his deep voice terribly off key. The others were singing along, even Mr. Carter, but it was obvious they didn't know what the hell they were saying. The goofy goalie could have been leading them in a song where they were calling themselves asswipes. Laughing hazel eyes met mine as I walked to my stupid cat picture. I might give it to Harper. She really loved that cat. "Walker. Come sing the cleanup song with us!"

I shook my head. I have no idea how this happened, but I found myself mumbling along as I washed my brushes. The stink of turpentine made my nose wrinkle. Mr. Carter appeared at my side, and I handed him the wet brushes.

"I'm glad to see your headache has eased up."

"Yeah, it's manageable. They say coffee helps with migraines, so I thought, what the hell, might as well have a cup." He nodded softly and moved on. My sight stayed on him even when the other men were heading out the door. I stamped along behind them, with Mr. Carter walking at my side, his shorter legs working twice as hard to keep up. I slowed down. "You got a first name?" I asked and got an amused look in reply.

"Most people do," he answered as we waited for the red hand to turn green.

"Think you might want to tell me what it is?" I asked, hands in my coat pockets, palms suddenly sweaty.

FOUR

Finn
_____

I WASN'T USUALLY IN THE HABIT OF WITHHOLDING MY
first name from my adult students. After all, there was
enough "Mr. Carter" in my day job to make me
shudder at hearing it after hours, but stepping into a
chaotic room had sent my walls shooting sky-high.

It wasn't just the overturned chairs or the canvas
boards tossed around like litter. Bob, a hulking figure,
had his large hand wrapped tightly around Arnaud's
throat, face red, veins standing out in anger. Arnaud's
eyes were wild, and dark curses slipped from his lips
in rapid-fire French. Chip was stimming in panic. Taft
being lean and jittery, tried to get them apart, but his
fingers, twitching, were caught somewhere between
wanting to intervene and bolting from the room
entirely.

And then there was Walker.

He'd been apart from it all, arms crossed, exuding a kind of quiet control even amid the bedlam. His brown eyes had fixed on me when I froze in the doorway, and for a moment, I'd felt pinned by his stare, which made my pulse quicken. There was a silent dominance in his posture and his sharp gaze, and when he'd gotten in front of Bob, it derailed the big man's temper in an instant. He'd radiated authority like he was used to being listened to without question.

His presence alone had settled things, the tension visibly draining from Bob's clenched fists and the wild panic fading from Taft's eyes.

He was so capable, and I had a competency kink.

Sue me.

Now, he waited at the stoplight with me. The others having already made it over, hooting and hollering like a bunch of kids. Walker was tall enough that I had to tip my head back to meet his eyes.

"And?" he prompted.

I hesitated again, feeling unexpectedly vulnerable, my pulse quickening with uncertainty. Why was I withholding my name and turning this simple exchange into some odd game? Walker had unsettled me in ways I hadn't anticipated, stripping away layers of practiced confidence I thought I'd perfected since my awkward teenage years. Maybe it was the intensity of his gaze or the gentle sincerity behind his rough exterior. A man who'd sketched a cat and quietly spoke of affection as something earned rather than freely given. He made me question my carefully constructed defenses. Something about Walker had gotten under my skin, but equally, this attraction—if that is what it was—reminded me of moments in my past when I'd trusted someone a little too quickly, only to regret it later.

So, I deflected.

"Why didn't you break up the fight?" I blurted out, unable to stop the question hovering on my tongue.

Walker shrugged slightly, looking almost casual about it. "Bob and Arnaud?" he asked as if there might have been another fight. "I did break it up."

"A bit too late." I huffed. "They'd been at it a while, but one word from you, and they parted like a cheap wig in a windstorm."

He fought a smirk. Asshole. "That's hockey. Coach comes in. The fighting stops. But it doesn't mean there won't be fighting."

"That's ridiculous."

"Look, they do their thing; I do mine."

I frowned, not entirely convinced. "So, you don't mind your friends beating each other up?"

He winced, a brief shadow passing through his eyes. "They're not my friends," he said quietly, his voice edged with something distant and guarded.

"Teammates, then."

He crossed his arms over his impressively muscular chest, his biceps flexing briefly beneath the fabric of his shirt. And no, I wasn't looking.

Or I wasn't trying to, but jeez…

His expression hardened slightly, a mix of stubborn determination and guarded vulnerability flickering across his face. "Not my teammates for long," he said firmly. Then, he lifted one hand, tapping two fingers against his temple in a casual but revealing gesture. "Fix what's up here, and I'm gone. Back to where I belong."

"And that is?"

"Back to the Vipers."

The Vipers were hockey. The New York Vipers. Yep, that sounded like a thing. Sports and I were not a thing. I left that up to my brother with his jock genes, but I wasn't born under a rock either, and I'd seen games. "Hockey is mostly fighting, right?" I provoked.

"Not *all* fighting, you know."

"Well, I guess not, given you have to score touchdowns." I was going for tongue-in-cheek, but he looked horrified.

"Goals," he sputtered.

"And you have to get the bouncy ball through the teeny-tiny basket, right?"

He narrowed his gaze, and I couldn't help but smile. After a moment, he returned the smile. "Yeah, yeah, we get the touchdowns in the baskets."

"And fight," I added with a nod.

"So much fighting," he deadpanned. The lights changed, and we crossed over. For a second, he had his hand on my lower back, encouraging me to cross, looking out for God knows what hazards so he could —oh, I don't know—swoop in. I stopped him with a hand on his arm when we reached the sidewalk.

"My name is Finn," I said finally, and the admission felt strangely vulnerable, as though I'd handed him a secret instead of just my name.

"Finn," he repeated, testing it out, lips quirking slightly at the corners. "Suits you."

"Thanks," I said awkwardly, then added, half-jokingly, half-seriously, "it's not a big secret. Just not used to stepping into fight clubs disguised as art classes."

He chuckled, a warm, low sound that made

something pleasantly tighten in my chest. "I wish I could be sorry, but hockey players have too much testosterone, not enough sense."

"Apparently," I agreed, sneaking a sideways glance at him. Walker wasn't just attractive in an ordinary way. He was attractive in a monumental, almost intimidating manner, like a mountain you'd admire from a distance but never imagine climbing. Broad shoulders that looked strong enough to support the weight of the world, eyes that held storms and secrets, and that casual strength that made it impossible not to notice him.

I shook off the distracting thoughts as we fell into a comfortable silence, entering Mabel's Donut Shop. The others had already gathered at a table in the far corner. Arnaud was at the counter, taking charge of ordering in French, accompanied by vigorous hand gestures toward the increasingly bewildered barista.

"Is it wise putting Arnaud in charge?"

"He's extremely particular about his coffee," Walker deadpanned, guiding me gently toward the table with that same maddeningly casual touch to my lower back. Warmth radiated from his palm, making me overly aware of his nearness. When we reached the table, Walker gave Bob a firm tap on the shoulder, leaning in slightly with effortless authority. "Go rescue the poor barista before Arnaud traumatizes them. Black coffee for me, and two of those glazed crullers—the big ones."

I waited for Bob to lose his shit, expecting at least a grumble or a glare, but instead, he turned to me. "What you want, Teach?" Bob asked and glanced at the board and the somewhat frantic barista still struggling to interpret Arnaud's enthusiastic and entirely French coffee order.

"I'll have a vanilla latte and one of those maple-glazed crullers, please."

I pulled out my wallet, but Walker stopped me. "Bob's treat for losing his shit," he said and glanced at Bob as if daring him to disagree.

"Yeah, 'course, Teach. My bad," Bob said gruffly, his expression settling back into its usual irritated frown as he trudged over to Arnaud. He stood there, arms crossed defensively, grumbling quietly under his breath as Arnaud continued enthusiastically ordering coffee, oblivious to Bob's increasingly grumpy demeanor.

I slid into the chair, and Walker sat beside me, making the space feel even smaller with his imposing presence. Taft settled quietly on my other side, his hands folded carefully in his lap, scanning the room with a guarded interest. He seemed cautious and reserved even in this relaxed setting as if he was constantly measuring his environment and calculating how much of himself it was safe to show. Despite his quiet demeanor, Taft's intensity suggested he missed very little.

Watching him, I considered the art session earlier and what I'd learned so far, remembering each player's canvas. Bob's painting had been all sharp lines and dark, angry reds, mirroring his constant simmering irritation. Arnaud's had been chaotic yet vibrant, full of impulsive energy much like the man himself. Chip hesitated at every brushstroke, his uncertainty clearly showing in his sparse details, as though he feared making a mistake would cost him dearly. Taft's canvas had been precise, careful, and subtly expressive, each stroke purposeful yet restrained. The only artwork I hadn't yet analyzed was Walker's, but that would require more thought, and I wasn't quite ready to unpack everything he stirred in me.

Now was the time for quiet, informal, non-specific discussions built gently upon our art session's breakthroughs. But all my practiced opening lines vanished from my head because Walker's closeness was almost overwhelming. He was like a magnetic field, pulling at my focus until all I could think about was how his knee accidentally brushed mine under the table and how ridiculously aware I was of every inch of him.

"Can I ask you a question, Mr. Carter?" Chip asked tentatively, his expression earnest but cautious.

"Finn," I corrected gently, offering a reassuring smile. "Call me Finn."

"Okay, Finn," he said, visibly relaxing. "Do you paint yourself?"

"Of course he does not paint himself, Petit Chip," Arnaud cut in with a playful, heavily accented tone, sliding smoothly into his seat and nudging Chip firmly into the corner. "If he did, we would all see the paint everywhere—hands, hair, clothes." He waved dramatically, smiling broadly. "Mais peut-être, our Finn, he cleans up very nicely, non?"

Chip went scarlet.

"I know what he meant," I reassured. "I paint in my spare time when I'm not teaching first grade or working on my post-grad."

He sat forward in his chair. "Can you draw anything you look at? I have a friend who can do that."

"I wish. I'm more of an abstract artist, though I sometimes paint landscapes. But I love drawing caricatures." Taft blinked at me. "You know, like cartoon impressions of people. Hang on." I reached into my backpack and pulled out a marker pen, then grabbed a napkin from the holder, hesitating for a moment before sketching a quick doodle of Chip, capturing his mop of unruly curls and wide, eager eyes. When I turned it around, Chip's eyes widened even further, and the table erupted into comments.

"Oh, that's totally you!" Taft said, elbowing Chip in the side.

Arnaud leaned forward eagerly, tapping the table. "Now me, mon ami! You must capture my devastatingly 'andsome features."

Walker watched quietly, never demanding one of his own. I felt oddly at ease as I quickly sketched the others in turn. Arnaud's cocky smirk, along with the Band-Aid over his cut, Taft's thoughtful eyes, and Bob's bullish features. The arrival of coffee and crullers temporarily distracted everyone, pushing the sketches aside as hands eagerly reached for cups and pastries. The crullers vanished alarmingly fast. I'd barely taken two bites of my maple-glazed one before noticing the plate was empty except for crumbs. Walker's glazed crullers disappeared quickly, the speed almost impressive, while Arnaud and Bob wolfed theirs down in a way that suggested they hadn't eaten in days.

And there I was, having thought these guys would be anything like the bullies I'd known in school: cold, ruthless, and aggressive. Instead, they were a bunch of testosterone-driven teddy bears, each with their own set of vulnerabilities carefully hidden behind muscle and bravado.

Finally, I glanced up at Walker, pen poised. "Your turn."

He gave a slow, challenging smile, leaning in even closer. His brown eyes caught the warm glow of the coffee shop lights. "Make it good, Finn," he said. His deep voice made my pulse race and my cheeks flush slightly under the intensity of his gaze.

What the actual fuck?

I started sketching, my pulse quickening as I carefully traced the strong line of his jaw, the confident slope of his nose, and the faint, teasing curve of his lips. His eyes never left my face, making it increasingly difficult to maintain my composure. When I finally finished, I glanced up, feeling more exposed than expected.

"Done," I said softly, pushing the napkin toward him, unsure whether my rapid heartbeat was due to nerves or the closeness of his presence.

"Ah, Finn, you have made a silk purse from the ugly ear of the big pig!" Arnaud announced.

"Fuck you and the ugly-eared pig you rode in on," Walker said, which made no sense, then he took the drawing from me before folding it carefully and putting it in his pocket. "Mine," he murmured.

If only.

FIVE

Walker

WEIRDNESS.

My head was filled with it. Rolling away from the sun glaring through my window the next morning, I plucked the napkin with the cartoonish impression of me from the nightstand to stare at the sketch. Finn really did have talent. Much more than I could claim. I studied the drawing, wondering if this was truly how he saw me. Did he think I was attractive? I mean, seriously, this could be a sketch of Patrick Schwarzenegger.

I'd looked at my mug in enough mirrors to know I was not this good-looking. What generally stared back at me from a looking glass was some fucked-up version of a paranoid kid trying to keep meaty fists from landing on his baby sister.

The napkin floated back to the nightstand as I caught the not-so-light tread of Harper stepping up to my door. She knocked like a marine gunnery sergeant. Barked out orders like one too.

"Hey, you have a therapy session," she shouted through the door. How one little woman who barely came up to my chest and weighed a hundred pounds with her combat boots on could be so damn loud was a question for the ages.

"I'm up. Make some coffee." I sat up, rubbed my eyes, and waited.

"I'm not your maid, you know," Harper snapped back, then left. She would make coffee. Mine was undrinkable. So yeah, she totally had the coffee situation in hand. I kicked off the covers, pulled on some sweats, and took a second to gently fold the napkin into a tiny square and tucked it into my wallet, right between a condom and lube packets. Opening the door, I picked up the aroma of dark brew and maple oatmeal. As usual, Harper was singing along to some punk rock slash darkwave slash goth rock.

No one had ever been happier than Harper Jean Walker when the *Wednesday* series debuted. My sister had been a dark goddess ever since she was old enough to apply black lipstick. Dad hated all the goth crap, which made her embrace it even more. We'd not get into the many nights he'd lashed out at her for looking like a zombie slut, and I'd taken the blow meant for her. No point digging that shit up now. I could save it for the team-appointed therapist and tell him. He lived for that kind of trauma.

After a fast piss, I washed my hands, rubbed my fingers through my hair, and called it good. There was no reason to shower. I'd come home and wash off the session in a long, hot bath. Sometimes, old memories stick to your skin like leeches.

She was bouncing to an old Sisters of Mercy song, and I reached for her phone to turn down the music. Deep brown eyes, the same shape and color as mine, flew from the hot water she was pouring over her bowl of instant oatmeal.

"Dickhead move," she said, then shoved the bowl at me.

"We've been here for like a month, and the neighbors have already given us shit about the noise." I nudged her bony hip with mine. She smiled with pride. "Yeah, no, don't smile. We're supposed to be walking a straight line here, Sprite."

She grimaced at the pet name, but deep down, she liked it. "Fine, I'll keep it down."

She totally wouldn't. I had to respect that kind of dedication to being a rebel. That came from growing up fighting. Something we both were experts at. Only thing was, Harper channeled her aggression into healthy things like kickboxing. She was so good she landed a job at one of the local gyms on the same day she applied, teaching a new class to the members. The various WIBA tournaments she had won here in the States, as well as in the Caribbean, had been a large part of her fast hire after moving. Also, and this is just me, but I think the guy who owns the gym was crushing on her. Not that he stood a chance, but hey, if he wanted to hit on her while hiding his wedding band in his desk drawer, he could. Harper brooked no bullshit from men. Another carryover from our childhood, I was sure.

"Can you drop me off at the rink?" I asked. She nodded, wavy black bangs falling into her eyes. "Your roots are showing." I tapped her head with my spoon.

"I know." She swatted the spoon away. "I'll touch them up tonight. How was the art class? Did you paint smiley skies and harmonious trees?"

"No, we painted happy things from our childhood." She grimaced. "Right? So, I did find one thing that made me less stabby. It's in the hall closet. It's for you. Hang it up on the wall next to that poster of Jenna Ortega."

The little shit dashed off, bowl of creamy oats in

hand. I waited while wearing a smile. Harper squealed. She had never outgrown that little-kid glee over a gift. Probably because we didn't get many as children. Even at twenty-two, she always got excited over the smallest present, which was why I tried to gift them to her as often as possible.

"Okay, I love this so much!" she exclaimed as she thundered back into the kitchen with the oil of that old cat in her hand. "It looks just like her."

"It looks like some asshole on brain meds painted it," I tossed out and got a pout. "I'm glad you like it."

"I love it." She placed it on the counter. "Did you enjoy the mandated art class?"

"Meh," I said, then spooned some oats into my mouth.

"Well, I think it's a good thing. Expressing yourself in ways that don't get twinks beat up."

"Says the woman who kicks people in the face for a living." She flexed a thin arm. "It's okay. Better than some other shit the team could have dreamed up." I glanced at my phone on the counter. "Shit, we better get going. Dr. Quackers is coming in early to meet me so I can watch morning skate."

"Okay, give me ten." Off she went, painting in one hand and oatmeal bowl in the other. I peeled off in the other direction to dress. In under ten, we were outside, the cold wind slapping us in the face as we made our way across the parking lot of our apartment complex. It was a nice place, right on the lake, but mother*fuck* was it cold. Not that we were beach babes or anything. We'd grown up in Newton, New Jersey, so we knew cold. This was a whole different level, though—probs because of the lake. I wasn't sure I wanted to live through some of the big snows they had here in Rochester, but I guessed there was no escaping them.

FIFTEEN MINUTES LATER, I STOOD OUTSIDE THE Rochester Energy Cooperative Arena, watching my sister speed off in my vehicle. Someone might as well drive it. She enjoyed tearing up the roads in my dark blue Ford F-150 Raptor. The tiny little woman sitting on a pillow in that massive pickup always made me snicker.

The titters withered up as I made my way through the rink. The crisp bite of cold rink air did little to ease the tension creeping up the back of my neck. The other players weren't here yet, though the coaches probably were. I did my best to avoid any staff as I slipped down the corridors past the weight room, dressing room, and laundry facilities. The door to the mental health counselor sat open, with the aroma of honey wafting out of the room.

Bracing myself, I pushed in to scan the counselor's office. If you judged the rest of the rooms that we hockey players utilized daily, this one would be as far from those as humanly possible. There was no sense of sport anywhere. Instead of the team colors of gold and black slathered everywhere, the walls had been painted a soft peach, with soft blue and green curtains, chairs, and throw rugs adorning the space.

Sitting in one of the chairs was Dr. Quackers, aka Dr. Milton Quackenbush. Age around fifty-five or so and gray whiskers shaped into a Sir Reginald Hargreeves from *The Umbrella Academy* series goatee. He wore slim, dark brown pants, a green sweater that looked like he knitted it himself—the sleeves were too long—and dino light-up high-top sneakers. There was a lot going on with the dude. A. Lot.

"Good morning, Walker. I was making tea. Would you like a cup? The honey is from a small farm just outside of town," Dr. Q asked, peering at me over his glasses. My sight darted to a little tea set on a round coffee table. A flowery teapot, two cups, a teensy creamer, itty-bitty spoons, and sugar cubes complete with silver tongs. And of course, the honey in a white and blue pottery honey pot.

"Sure." Why not. At least it gave me something to do with my mouth and hands. I flopped down opposite him as he poured. It would have been charming in a proper British way if we were British. We were not. I was Jersey-born—my accent and attitude were a dead giveaway—and Old Doc Quackers was straight out of Flatbush. His accent gave him away. His attitude? For a guy who grew up in Brooklyn with the name Quackenbush? Nah. That didn't jibe. He was way too Zen.

"You ever get beat up as a kid for having a last name that is so easy to make fun of?" I asked as he passed over a cup of dark red tea. "What kind of tea is this?"

He let the query about his name fly by. I was coming to learn he was not easy to rile.

"It's Rooibos tea. It's a lovely herbal blend with some tender notes of an earthy flavor, naturally caffeine-free and rich in antioxidants. It's also purported to aid in weight loss." He patted his little belly through his sweater. "I'm trying to drop a few pounds."

"Ah. Cool." I sipped the hot tea. Not bad. Not coffee by any means, but whatever. Thinking of coffee made me recall Finn, and just for a second, things felt a little lighter.

"So, now we're settled in with our tea and some lovely Tibetan bowl music in the background, why don't we discuss the past few days?"

"You go first." I jerked my chin at him.

He smiled at me over his cup of red tea. "Well, yesterday I spent time with my daughter and her son. We went to the library for drag story hour, then had lunch at a little café with amazing stromboli. Afterward, we went to a matinee movie."

"Very *Leave it to Beaver*," I commented, then sipped.

"Well, I'm no Ward, but I try my best." He briefly stared at his drink before bringing cool gray eyes back to me. "What have you done with yourself since we met last Friday?"

"Skated, battled headaches, went to that art class you suggested." I made air quotes around "suggested." To the Vipers organization, "suggested" translated to "mandatory." His eyes lit up. He was pleased. I shouldn't really care, but there was this kid's voice that belonged to little Walker, who was happy to have made this older man happy. "I painted a picture. Then, I flirted with the teacher. He made sketches of all of us."

"Oh, now that *is* a busy night of art. What did you paint?" He leaned up as if he were really interested in what I had to say. He probably wasn't. Poor guy had to sit here and listen to hockey players with mental health issues prattle on all day long. But he was getting paid the big bucks to act as if he gave a shit, so a little fake interest was to be expected.

"A cat." I sipped and stared at him.

"Was it a special cat?"

I shrugged. "To my sister it was."

"But not to you?"

My sight fell to the reddish tea in my cup. A few dark specks were floating around in the steaming liquid.

"She was a nice cat. Harper fed her scraps and snuck her into her room on good days."

"I'm glad for Harper, but what about you? Did you like the cat?"

"She was a nice cat."

"Did she have a name?"

Man, this was getting too close to shaky ground. "Yeah." I dipped my finger into the tea to try to push the floaters down, but the water was too hot to leave it in there. "Harper called her Spearmint because she lived in a nearby field and spent a lot of her time rolling around in a patch of spearmint, we guessed, because she always smelled like chewing gum."

"That's a good name for a cat."

"Yeah, she was a nice cat."

He sipped softly, silently, giving me time to sort the shit in my head. My gut was tight now as memories I'd tried to keep buried clawed their way to the fore.

"Would you feel safe in telling me more about Spearmint?"

"She died. Dad... well, our yard wasn't safe for cats." And there it was. Trauma. Lying there on my lap as if I'd coughed it up like a phlegm ball. Fuck. "Harper didn't know. I buried her and told Harper she got hit by a car."

He touched my hand. My sight flew from the imaginary glob of past horror to my counselor, and then, to his hand. He held tissues. My teacup began to shake. Shit. I hadn't even felt the tears chilling my face.

"Shit, sorry. That was... wow, this tea is making me weepy," I coughed as I sucked it up. All of it. No place for that kind of shit in hockey. Tears, snivels, boohooing over a long-dead pet. "I don't want any more."

I shoved the tea back at him. He wouldn't take it. The fucker.

"Is tea such a bad thing if it helps clear the soul of pains from our past?"

I had no answer, so I said nothing. I just sat there, wishing my head would stop hurting and dreaming of a bath to scour this all away. I thought to mention Finn to him, but that was a secret. It was good and sweet, and it was mine.

Keep the good things secret so no one can rip them away.

SIX

Finn
_____

I'D BEEN ANTICIPATING ART CLASS ALL WEEK. MAYBE
none of them would turn up. It wasn't mandatory, but
I still hoped they'd all show. I'd planned a session
introducing the color wheel through painting cartoon
birds, less about free expression than guided learning.
With my post-grad studies in mind, I was eager to put
it into practice, not just to gather supporting evidence
but because I genuinely believed this approach could
help.

That was why I was excited.

It had nothing to do with Walker and whatever
complicated feelings had been creeping in, like how
my pulse seemed to pick up whenever he was near or
how I found myself paying too much attention to the
curve of his mouth when he spoke. Attraction,

curiosity... or something I wasn't quite ready to name. The moments when he glanced my way, and his eyes lingered, stuck with me. I didn't know what to do with it, so I stuffed it down and told myself it didn't matter.

When I finally arrived, I was happy to see the five men huddled by the coffee machine, chatting quietly. "Hey, everyone," I called out, forcing my voice to sound casual. "Do you all have coffee? Has it been a good week?"

"Better now you're here, Prof," Arnaud teased, flashing a grin as he sauntered closer, his smile lingering just a second too long. His gaze flicked over me. Deliberate, assessing, and maybe even flirtatious. It caught me off guard, and I wasn't sure how to react. Was he just being playful, or was there something more? I found myself glancing toward Walker instinctively, wondering if he'd noticed or if he cared. The thought confused me, stirring something I wasn't ready to name. I smiled awkwardly at Arnaud and moved on, my heart still knocking harder than it should.

Bob frowned, his face set in a scowl as if I'd just interrupted something important. His jaw was tight, mouth pressed thin, as he'd rather be anywhere else.

"Stop fucking with Teach," Bob snapped at Arnaud. "Asshole."

"He is very pretty," Arnaud teased, and Bob glared. Taft and Chip hovered awkwardly. Taft kept shifting from foot to foot, his arms crossed tightly over his chest as if he was holding himself together. He flicked glances toward the door every few seconds, as though planning to run, while Chip lingered nearby, his gaze bouncing between the others, searching for a cue on how to act.

On the other hand, Walker scowled darkly, his arms overlapping as he moved his weight away from the group, eyes narrowing in Arnaud's direction. Was he irritated? Jealous? I couldn't tell, but something about his tense posture—the stiffness in his shoulders, and the way his jaw worked like he was grinding his teeth—felt different. I wondered whether Arnaud's teasing was bothering him or if something else was weighing him down. Either way, I made a mental note to check in with him later. At least no one was throwing punches this time.

Once everyone had coffee, I encouraged them to settle at their easels. "I want you to pick a light color, any color you like," I explained, grabbing a brush to demonstrate. "Add some water and paint me a blob right in the middle of the paper." I swirled the brush in a cup of water, tapped off the excess, and let a soft blue puddle bloom on the page. "Nothing fancy, just a starting point."

"A sexy blob?" Arnaud quipped, smirking as he dragged his brush across the paper in exaggerated curves.

"What kind of blob?" Taft asked, frowning in concentration as if there was a right answer.

"Any kind," I reassured him, walking behind them and checking their work as I moved. I offered quiet encouragement, adjusting a brush grip here and nudging a water cup away from the edge there.

Then I reached Walker. His blob stood out. A soft cotton candy pink, delicate and precise.

"Nice color," I said quietly, unsure if he'd acknowledge me. Walker's jaw tightened, but he didn't say anything.

"Now," I said, stepping back to the front of the room. "Let's pick another color. Something different this time. Brighter, darker, whatever you like." I grabbed another brush, dipped it in crimson, and added a second blotch to my paper, this one smaller and off to the side. "Go ahead and add your second blob somewhere else on the page. Think about how the colors work together, overlapping, blending, or sitting side by side. There's no wrong way to do it."

Arnaud grinned as he flicked his brush in lazy circles, muttering something about "sexy blobs" again, and Taft's brows knitted in focus as if he were calculating the perfect placement. Chip quietly followed along, carefully measuring out his brushstrokes. When I glanced back at Walker, I noticed his hand hovering above his paint, brush poised but still. He was staring at his first pink blob.

"Just go for it," I encouraged softly. "There's no right answer." Walker exhaled heavily, dipped his brush in purple, and added a second blob. It was smaller, tucked in like it didn't want to be seen.

"Shit," Bob muttered, and I stood behind him. "It fucking ran! It's all mixed."

"It's all good," I reassured. "See that?" I pointed to where the colors bled together. "That's called a bloom. It's what happens when wet paint hits a damp spot. You never quite know what you'll get. Sometimes, the paint dances across the page, making every accident beautiful."

"And happy," Arnaud said with a grin, adopting a soft, soothing tone as he channeled his best Bob Ross impression. "There are no mistakes, only happy little accidents." He exaggeratedly smiled and wiggled his fingers like he was conjuring magic. "Behold! My happy blob!" he declared dramatically.

A ripple of laughter followed. Even Taft chuckled under his breath. The tension that had clung to the room like static seemed to break, loosening the air. Walker's scowl softened just a little, his brush moving again, slow and deliberate.

We worked through the process of waiting for the paint to dry, how the colors lightened, and how the mixing worked. I was in my element as every man listened. As I moved around the room, I stopped by Walker's station, catching his faint scent beneath the tang of paint—something warm and earthy that made my breath hitch. He'd paused, brush hovering above his canvas, hesitating as if unsure where to place an eye on one of his abstract birds.

"Where?" he asked.

I touched his arm briefly. "Anything works," I murmured. "Just go for it." His shoulder tensed under my hand, but after a beat, he dipped his brush again, added a dark eye, and then glanced up at me for reassurance. "Great." I lingered for a second longer than needed before moving on.

The conversation about adding wings took on a life of its own. Bob grumbled that wings were too fiddly, muttering about how he'd mess it up. "Birds don't need wings if they're grounded," he declared firmly, like that settled it.

"Ah, c'est parce que vos oiseaux n'ont pas le courage de voler," Arnaud shot back with a wink, flicking a feathered flourish across his canvas with dramatic flair. "Yours do not fly! But mine? Ils volent. Regardez ça!" He swept his brush through the air like a conductor, pretending his paint strokes could carry the whole room skyward.

Bob snorted. "More like they're gonna crash and burn."

"That's passion." Arnaud grinned. "Even a crash is beautiful." He turned to me, gesturing at his chaotic creation. "Finn, tell Bob my birds are magnifique."

"They're definitely… energetic," I offered diplomatically, and Arnaud cackled, clearly pleased with himself. Even Bob couldn't hide the twitch of a smile.

Walker had lingered after the session ended, quietly helping clear the tables while the others shuffled out. I waited for him by the door, and together, we trailed the others to the coffee shop. Walker stayed quiet the whole way, with his hands in his pockets, shoulders slightly hunched as if carrying something heavy.

"How's everything going?" I asked when we reached the corner, my voice softer than I'd intended. Walker's silence had been heavy the whole way, and now, watching him walk as he was, I knew something was wrong.

"Okay," Walker said, then shook his head. "No." He shrugged, his voice flat. "Same shit, different day."

I hated that answer. It sounded like he'd stopped expecting things to improve. I paused, debating whether to push or let it go. "You wanna talk about it?" I asked, keeping my voice low. "I can just listen. No pressure."

He snorted softly. "What's there to say?"

"Maybe nothing," I admitted. "But sometimes saying nothing out loud can help."

He stared at the pavement like it had answers he couldn't find, his fingers twitching restlessly inside his pocket. "I just… " He sighed. "I'm tired. Feels like every day I'm running uphill and never getting anywhere."

"Yeah," I said quietly. "That sounds hard." I didn't push or ask for more. I just stood beside him.

"Thanks," he muttered eventually. It wasn't much, but I knew what it cost him to say it. For now, I'd take it.

I ended up next to Walker again, and when he shifted slightly, his arm brushed mine, and for a second, I thought he'd pull away. Instead, he leaned in a little, his weight settling closer. I didn't know what it meant—if it meant anything—maybe he was looking for a connection, but it didn't mean there was anything between us.

Not that there could be.

Still, I let myself stay there, not speaking to him, just sitting in the comfort of his quiet presence as we listened to Arnaud harassing the barista in French again with Bob beside him, elbowing his side.

"Will you draw us again, this time in our team colors?" Taft asked, then slid over a box of colored pencils and an art pad, clearly prepared.

"You shouldn't ask that," Walker warned. "He's off the clock—"

"It's okay," I cut him off, reassuring him. "I love art."

I glanced at Walker, and he immediately dropped his gaze. Where was confident Walker? What happened since last week?

I picked up a pencil and began sketching light, swift lines to capture the way Taft hunched in on himself, Arnaud's exaggerated pout, Chip's crooked smile, and Bob's ever-present scowl. The others drifted closer, crowding around the table, leaning in with interest, offering comments like we were all just killing time at a diner instead of sitting in mandatory team therapy.

"Make my hair cooler," Arnaud joked, fluffing the already perfect wave that flopped artfully across his forehead.

"You wish," Bob teased.

Arnaud didn't miss a beat. "Come on, Bob. You've got two settings: scowl and rage. Maybe I can lend you a hair product or a personality."

Bob snorted. "Don't need product when your head's already full of hot air."

"Oh, please," Arnaud shot back, still smiling, but his eyes had gone sharp. "Is this about earlier? You still mad because I made you look in touch with your feelings for five seconds?"

"Keep pushing, Arnaud," Bob warned, his voice low, jaw working as if he was grinding down the edge of something sharper. "See how that works out for you."

Arnaud leaned in, resting an elbow on the table. "I'm just saying, maybe if you stopped treating every conversation like a fistfight, someone might actually like you."

"Better to be real than fake," Bob snapped. "People see right through your charm. Hell, they probably see through you."

The table went quiet. Even Taft froze mid-laugh, eyes wide.

I kept my pencil moving, pretending not to feel the air thicken between them, tension coiled like a spring.

And then Chip, bless him, mumbled, "Statistically, conflict during group art therapy results in a 27 percent decrease in perceived emotional safety. Just saying."

There was a beat of silence.

Taft choked on a laugh.

Arnaud blinked, then pulled back, hands raised in mock surrender. "See? The science is against you, Bob."

Bob grumbled something under his breath but said nothing.

Crisis averted. For now.

Walker stayed back, arms crossed, watching quietly. His gaze wasn't on the paper but on me, eyes hooded as if lost in thought. The others drifted away, tired from the day's class, but Walker remained.

"How do you want me to draw you?" I asked, hoping to coax him into something lighter, easier

Walker blinked, clearly caught off guard, eyes wide, when he realized it was just the two of us at the table. "I don't know," he said slowly. "Like… me, I guess."

"Okay," I said softly, but I didn't begin the sketch immediately. "You serious, though? Because I can draw you heroic like a Marvel poster or mysterious like one of those shadowy noir guys." I paused, pretending to assess him with an exaggerated squint. "Or, you know, super casual: hoodie, coffee cup, that whole moody vibe you've got going."

The corner of his mouth twitched—almost a smile —and tension seemed to ease from his shoulders. "I guess… moody sounds about right."

"Got it," I said, grinning as I reached for a dark pencil. Then, I hesitated and swapped it for a brown one, which was the exact shade of Walker's incredible eyes.

I started with the outline, sketching light and loose to capture the shape of his face, the sharp cut of his jaw, and the faint crease between his brows that never seemed to fully disappear. I let my pencil soften when I reached his mouth, rounding the edges to suggest something gentler—the hint of a smile he rarely showed. Then, I moved to his eyes, carefully layering delicate strokes with the cocoa pencil, shading just enough to reflect how his gaze seemed to hold too much: frustration, exhaustion, or something quieter and harder to name. With a few strokes to capture his hair, I set the pencil down, suddenly nervous, and pushed it toward him.

He picked it up, and his frown was back. "Is this... how you see me?" Walker asked quietly, his gaze fixed on the page. "I don't look moody."

I huffed a soft laugh. "No," I admitted. "You look a little sad with the pretty... but that's okay."

His eyes widened, startled, like I'd said something that knocked him off balance. His gaze flicked away sharply, and for a second, I thought he might say something. His mouth opened, but no words came out. Whatever thought he was holding back, he swallowed it down and gave a stiff shrug instead. "Yeah... okay."

I checked my watch. It's not that I needed to be anywhere, but I had reviews to write for today and wanted to get to them while the session was still fresh in my head. Still, I lingered, feeling the weight of Walker's presence beside me.

"You wanna go for a walk?" he asked, his voice lower than usual as if asking for company was unfamiliar. He rubbed the back of his neck and shifted his weight. "No pressure, but... it's snowing and... "

I glanced out the window. Snow? Wow, so it was.

"Sure," I said, hiding my surprise. "That sounds nice."

His shoulders relaxed a little, and he gave a tight smile before stuffing his hands into his pockets. We walked quietly. It was snowing lightly—more of a suggestion than actual snow—faint specks swirling in the air and clinging to our coats. The wind cut sharp and bitter through the dark, slicing past the corners of the buildings and right into us. The cold nipped at my cheeks and stung my ears, but somehow, walking beside Walker, it didn't feel unpleasant. Our steps fell into an easy rhythm, boots crunching against the thin dusting of snow gathering on the sidewalk.

"There's a park I go to sometimes, just up here," Walker said.

"Is there? I don't know this area well."

"Do you want to see?"

"Sounds good."

We reached the park's entrance beneath a wrought iron sign reading Darcy Arbor Park that hung over the gate, and followed a path that snaked between skeletal trees. Walker slowed, his breath curling in front of him like smoke.

"I like the art class... " he started, then stopped. He swallowed hard and, then, resumed walking.

"I'm so pleased."

He shot me a half-smile, albeit brief, almost hesitant. "Can I ask you something?"

"Always."

"What does the art I make mean to you?"

"Mean?"

He stopped walking again, tugging me closer to the trunk of the nearest tree, shielding us from the wind. His fingers lingered on my sleeve a second longer than necessary before he let go.

"I choose pastels," he said, his voice softer now, like he was unsure where the words were leading. "I like pink and lilac and… I don't know, softer colors. Some people say that's weird." He paused, swallowing hard, his gaze fixed on the dark stretch of empty path ahead.

"My favorite color is purple," I said.

"You can get away with purple," he mused. "It's strong, you know? But when I use the lighter colors… it feels gentle. Is that wrong?"

I smiled softly. "Art is never wrong, and color therapy is a thing, you know."

"Yeah?" He let out a breath, almost like he'd been holding it in. "I don't know… sometimes I think if I make things soft enough, I can forget all the… " His words faltered again. He shook his head like he was frustrated with himself. "Forget it."

"No," I said quietly. "I get it. You want to create something safe."

He looked at me then. Something fragile flickered behind his guarded expression. "Yeah," he said, barely above a whisper. "Something safe."

We walked on, side by side, his arm brushing mine again. This time, neither of us pulled away.

By the time we made it back to my car, he was messaging someone to pick him up. I wasn't going to cross a line and offer to drive him somewhere. I waved as I drove away, glancing back at him, seeing his hand lift and return the wave.

Next week couldn't come soon enough.

SEVEN

Walker

SNOW. IT FELL LIGHTLY AS I SHUFFLED MY WAY DOWN the sidewalk to the community center, flakes tumbling downward in a little ballerina frost fairy dance as Harper used to call snowfall. I paused, looked left and right, and then behind me to ensure my sister had pulled off before falling to one knee to run my finger through the cold white dust on the cement walkway. There was little wind roaring off the lake tonight, a blessing, as the temps had tumbled now December had arrived. The snow was cold, delicate like Chantilly lace, and melted instantly. Funny how we never take the time to enjoy snow as adults. As kids, we loved it. As grown-ups? Not so much. It's a hassle to shovel, it makes driving hazardous, and it cancels school if you get enough, which is a PITA for working parents. Great for kids, but a headache for adults.

I guess that was part of leaving childhood behind. I drew a circle on the sidewalk, then filled it in to complete a smiley face. A pair of soft blue sneakers came into sight. My gaze flew up from my impromptu artwork to my art teacher. Finn. He was smiling down at me.

"Hey," I gruffly said, rising and moving my foot over the smiley snow face to clear it from existence. Maybe there was something to be said for leaving childish things in the past.

"Hey," he replied, hugging himself tightly as flakes fell softly onto his hair and lashes, dotting his cheeks. I reached up to brush one off his nose. His eyes widened.

"You're early." He took a step back. My hand fell. I felt like a moron for being so brazen.

"Yeah, my sister had to be at the gym. She teaches kickboxing." I walked around him, shoulders tight, my hand gripping the small package in my coat pocket. This whole season was stupid. The fact I'd allowed Harper to suck me into all the ho-ho-ho bullshit I blamed on the mood stabilizers. Not since I'd left home had I allowed a tree in the house or lights or silly window peels of reindeer and elves.

Fucking elves. If Santa and his little minions were so magical, why hadn't they done something to help me and my sister? Yep, just like God, they sat by and watched with their thumbs up their rumps.

"Wow, that's impressive! Is she good?" He trailed along after me, jogging to get to my side. I yanked the door open and held it, all courtly gentleman, for him. He gave me a tiny smile as he darted inside.

"She could kick my ass on any given night."

His eyes flared. "That *is* impressive."

"She rocks. Best human being on the planet, bar none."

"I have a brother," he said as we made our way down to the art room, the halls empty, our footfalls falling into a matched rhythm as I slowed for him. "He's one of my favorite people on the planet as well."

I nodded and stopped in front of a bulletin board covered with flyers for local craft fairs, holiday events, and Christmas concerts. There was so much red and green that I had to look elsewhere. Like at Finn, who was much prettier than any jingle bell or gaudy glass ball stickers.

"Is your brother a teacher too?" I asked simply because I wanted to know more about the man. Sue. Me.

"No, he's an electrician." He padded around me as he talked. I enjoyed the way the lights made his hair look highlighted. "He doesn't have the patience for teaching."

He entered the art room, me on his heels, breathing in the aroma of his cologne.

"Yeah, teachers need a lot of that." I peeled off my coat, taking care not to jar the little gift in my pocket. When I'd seen it online, it had seemed the perfect present for a guy who made me feel lighter than a dandelion blow, but now it was time to maybe hand it over, it felt stupid. Overly emotional. Feminine. Gay. Fag.

Ah, *there* was Dad. He'd been silent for a few weeks. Probably a combination of the meds, sitting with Dr. Quackers three times a week, and coming here to paint blobs and birds and long-dead cats. I'd not missed him in my head.

"Sometimes, yes, we do." He chuckled warmly. I turned to find him leaning on the edge of the old metal desk, his eyes glowing with the love he had for his profession. "Teaching is a calling. We're not getting rich. It's getting to know your students and their families and leading them in a direction for enrichment. It's way more than getting your class to learn their ABCs and one, two, threes. You have to listen to the subtle hints they give you to help them blossom and learn to the best of their abilities."

"Wish I had a teacher who had listened," I mumbled, lost in his beauty. When his expression shifted from affection to concern, I bit the inside of my cheek. Stupid. "But I had good coaches. Lots of them."

"Good, that's good. I'm glad you had such admirable adults to help teach you." He seemed a little flustered now, probably because I was as well. I tended to project hostility when I got upset, according to several dozen people.

"Yeah, so, uhm… " I now hated the fact we were here alone. Just a few minutes ago, I was glad to have all of his attention. Shit, I was touching snowflakes on his little button nose. Now, I wanted to dive through the window. "So, yeah, I think we should get some of those donuts with the fancy holiday icing on them tonight."

He blinked. "Oh, donuts, yes, that would be nice. I'm hoping to do a holiday-themed class tonight with lots of seasonal colors and frivolity. Maybe paint some toys from our childhoods that we remember fondly."

"My toys were all misfits," I tossed out, hoping for a laugh. Finn seemed confused. "Like that old

Rudolph show with the island filled with toys that no kids wanted?"

"Oh yes, of course. I always loved that little elf who dreamed of being a dentist."

"I liked Bumble."

He snickered as he looked up at me. I liked the way the lines around his hazel eyes crinkled when he smiled.

"I can see that," he teased, just lightly, but it was enough to show me he had a sense of humor, gentle as it was, under all that pretty.

He put me at ease—something few people other than my sister and my therapist could do. He was special. Sweet. Tender.

"I saw this thing online last week—" I began to say, but then snapped my mouth shut as the other bozos rolled into class, joshing and shoving, and Arnaud singing what sounded like "Jingle Bells" in French.

Finn tipped his head as if waiting for me to continue. No way was I giving it to him with those butt-scratching baboons in the vicinity. They would make fun of me. Poke. Prod. Call me a girly boy.

"It was this farting fish," I hurried to lie. The others were instantly drawn to the farting fish conversation. Finn, being the teacher, got us into place in front of our easels while leading the discussion from flatulence to using different brushes to create diverse textures that would open us up to a wider range of emotions.

Nope. I was not emoting in front of my fellow Copperheads. Hockey players did not emote in such floofy ways. We knew only two emotions. Happiness when we won, and sadness when we lost. Oh, and anger. We knew three acceptable emotions. Anything else was for limp-wristed queers.

Ugh. Dad showed up at the worst times. Finn watched from behind me as I threw some colors on the canvas. Deep browns with a splash of green that I smeared about to look like a pine tree before slapping a glob of gold atop the ugly tree. Then, I slathered the words Merry Shitmas, which got a few snorts from the guys but only a look of concern from Finn.

Class was not fun at all that night. Coffee and donuts in a shop that was decorated to the damn rafters was not fun. Eating donuts with red and green icing was so very much not fun. I left early and walked to the nearest bus stop, snow falling at a goodly clip, and took a bus home.

My tiny present for Finn was still in my pocket. I ripped off the paper, then tore the small box into bits before I chucked it into the dumpster outside our complex.

I went inside, kicked the door shut, toed off my wet sneakers, removed my damp socks, and then raced to the window to stare down at the dumpster. An epic battle took place inside my head. Dad vs Walker. This time, amazingly, Walker won the fight and let himself feel things. Real things. Good things. Kind things. Things guys were allowed to feel…

"Fuck off, old man," I snarled to the lingering snarl of a man lying in his grave, yet still able to torment me. Shaking like a leaf, I threw the door open and ran back to the trash can, climbed inside, and pawed around until I located the little statue of a man holding an apple in one hand and a slate in the other that read "World's Best Teacher."."

I'll give it to him next week. No backing down. Holding the little ceramic figurine to my chest, my bare feet carried me into my apartment, and I placed it on my nightstand before unfolding the drawings Finn had made of us over the past few weeks. My ass found the floor. I drew my feet in to run the cold out of them and felt a serenity settle over me that had nothing to do with meds or facing down the demons that clung to me like burdocks.

"Next week," I vowed to the statuette.

FOUR DAYS AFTER THE SNOWY SMILEY FACE, I WAS sitting in the Copperheads video room, being a good little puck pusher, and watching vids of the team we were playing next. I came in daily, skated with the offensive coach -- a nice guy named Bill Pawlowski -- then worked out or watched videos. Due to the meds, I was not allowed to skate with the team. Or hadn't been. Last session, I had badgered Dr. Quackers to lower the restrictions to let me skate with the team. Even if it was just in a no-contact jersey. It was BS making us art boys -- as Arnaud was so thrilled to call us, like it was a damn after-school club -- fiddle with our schlongs as we worked out our shit.

"If I don't get back to doing the one thing I do well soon, I am going to go totally batshit," I confessed as he tugged on his pointy goatee while some sort of berry tea steeped. "I'm better. The side effects are less. I need to do something productive," I'd said as he studied his teapot as if he were expecting it to talk like that one in *Beauty and the Beast*. Yes, I knew all the Disney princesses. I'd grown up watching them with my little sister. Come at me, motherfuckers. Boys can enjoy singing candelabra.

"You don't find therapy productive?" he asked because of course he had.

I chuckled appreciatively. "Clever." I wagged a finger at him. He seemed pleased with himself. The whiskery jerk. "Yeah, of course it's productive, but I'm a hockey player. It's what I do. It's me. It's like asking… " I scoured my brain for an example. Amazingly or not, Finn popped up. "Like asking an artist not to paint when he's struggling through hard times."

"So, you express yourself on the ice?" he enquired, then leaned up to pour the tea. Fruity fumes tickled my nose. I nodded. "Do you plan to express yourself on the ice in an acceptable way or with your fists?"

"Doc, it's hockey. I mean, if someone runs my goalie, I will go after him. If someone cross-checks our best scorer, I will go after him. It's part of the game. But no, I won't do anything too violent unless someone asks for it."

He snickered softly. I cocked an eyebrow.

"I'm not sure that's the positive reply you seem to think it is, but I will consider running some tests."

He'd passed me a cup of coffee, and I had thanked him. And now here I am, watching videos after spending the morning on the ice with the team. It had been *everything*. I mean, Jesus H. Christ, it had been good. No one really knew me. They knew of me, obviously, but they'd all been decent. Chatting me up as if I'd not wailed on a phone-thieving twink like I was Georges St. Pierre just a few months ago. The ice had been crisp. The air brittle. I'd knocked a few pucks past the starting goalie, a bruising Russian named Matvey, who liked to call out derogatory animal names to people shooting at him.

"Your shot is weak like ferret piss."

"You are as feeble as a skinny weasel."

"Your slap shot is stinky like mink shit."

Mustelids seemed to be Matvey's mammal of choice. It was all good. He could call me a fucking smelly stoat all day if that made him happy. I was just thrilled to be on the ice, stick in hand, feeling I was doing something. Anything was better than sitting around my apartment as my sister worked, jerking off to mental images of Finn kissing his way down my dick as soap operas played in the background. Stir-crazy was a thing.

Yeah, things were okay. Not great. Not even close, but okay. My head still ached at times, and I was still peeling off mental scabs in therapy that bled for days afterward, but overall, life was okay. I could even look at the blue spruce in the corner of our living room and not be overwhelmed with the need to light it afire, then chuck it into the lake. Progress.

It was slow and hurt like an infected toe, but it was being made.

Now, all I had to do was work up the courage to give Finn his little gift.

It was beyond ridiculous for a big, tough asshole hockey player to be so scared to give a guy a present. Maybe there was something extra special about Finn that needed a little more time to cure or whatever word artists used to call a painting that was in progress. That was me. An unfinished oil. A maquette of a sculpture. A rough draft of a novel.

An incomplete man searching for the one to help make him whole.

EIGHT

Finn

By the time I stumbled through my front door, I was dead on my feet. I was covered in glitter, and my scarf had somehow managed to knot itself twice around my neck. I must have looked like I'd barely survived a festive ambush.

I wasn't surprised to hear the TV on. My brother had a key. He'd always had a key. A "just in case" key that turned into a "whenever I feel like eating your food and leaving socks on your couch" key. The smell of pepperoni and cheese drifted from the coffee table, and my stomach growled in response.

"How was school?" my brother, Connor, asked without looking away from the screen. Then, when he glanced up, he snorted a laugh. "Must be close to Christmas," he added.

"Too close."

"You're home late."

I dropped my bag by the door and shrugged out of my scarf. "School play rehearsal, then staff beers, where we discussed why the hell we decided to be teachers in the first place."

"N'awww, little kids and glitter, easy."

I huffed. "Fuck off, asshole. Imagine herding cats, if the cats were hopped up on candy canes and high on the promise of Santa."

"Bet you crushed it." He took a massive bite of pizza and pointed at the TV. "Vipers are down two, and it's only ten minutes in. Defense is a mess."

I kicked off my shoes, stumbled toward the couch, and flopped beside him. I knew I should've gone to my desk and started tackling the mountain of post-grad work waiting for me, but exhaustion won out. The play rehearsal had taken up the entire afternoon and had drained every ounce of my energy, not to mention the annual shit-we're-exhausted staff meeting with Principal Lewis. Besides, the pizza smelled too good to resist.

"Yeah? What's up with it?" I'm sure Walker plays defense. I could easily ask Connor, but then he'd want to know why I was asking, and the NDA I signed was a thing, and yeah… not happening because if my brother knew I was helping out hockey players, he'd combust with how big a fan he was of the New York team.

Not that Walker played for them anymore, given he was working for their feeder team now.

I grabbed a slice and took a bite. It was greasy and glorious.

"They lost a couple of guys, and now they're scrambling," Connor said, reaching for his beer. "Vipers used to be tight. Now, they can't hold a defensive zone to save their lives. Goalie's working overtime."

I barely understood half of what he was saying, but I kept asking questions—anything to put off my looming responsibilities. Something about the low hum of Connor's voice, the comfortable sprawl of the couch, and the warmth of pizza in my hands was easier than facing my towering to-do list.

"What if they just picked up someone else?" I asked. "Or used someone from their feeder team, the uhm… "

"The Copperheads."

"Who they gonna call up?" Connor asked as if I had any idea at all. "That's a team of fuck ups. Might as well skate with a traffic cone."

The urge to defend Walker was shockingly

instantaneous, but not far behind were Bob, Arnaud, Chip, and Taft. "Sounds dramatic," I said instead of saying anything about the guys I'd been doing art with for four weeks now.

"You know hockey." Connor grinned. "Drama's part of the package."

I chuckled and reached for another slice. My laptop and unfinished reports stayed cold and untouched on my desk. Tonight, hockey and greasy pizza were the only things on my schedule.

Oh, and I'm still wondering why I had this insane urge to defend the Copperheads.

But mostly Walker.

CONNOR STAYED OVER, BEMOANING THE VIPERS' defense and the state of his love life, and I was late to bed, early to rise, and now, running on fumes. Today, was just as busy as yesterday, and I still found glitter after two showers.

The wailing hit me first. Sharp, piercing, and unmistakably Polly Lexington's familiar cry. It's remarkable that only a couple of months into the academic year, I could already tell my class of six-year-olds apart just by their laughs or cries.

"He cut it! He cut it!" Polly shrieked, her voice

breaking with the kind of distress that only children can master—raw, unfiltered panic.

Polly was one of my more confident kids. The kind who called a spade a spade and wasn't afraid to cause a little upset if she thought she was in the right. But when I sprinted toward the playhouse, I hadn't expected to see her clutching her head.

Jamie stood nearby, sobbing, a pair of craft scissors in one hand and a thick hank of Polly's blonde hair in the other.

"What the h—" I caught myself. "Jamie," I said carefully. "Give me the scissors."

He held them out to me. They weren't school scissors, too sharp. They were the kind a parent might keep in a kitchen drawer. My stomach twisted. Had he brought them into school? We had every type of lockdown procedure, but did we need scanners for our six-year-olds? I took them and shoved them deep in my pocket.

Polly's face was blotchy and red, her hands gripping the uneven length where her bright blonde hair had been hacked away. Her cries hitched on gasps, snot smeared down her face, and her whole body shook with each shuddering breath. Jamie, meanwhile, held his ground as if he'd just won a prize.

"She said my hair was like a girl's," Jamie declared as if that explained everything. I turned to Mrs. Gilbert, our classroom assistant, a mom who volunteered every Monday; and asked her to get Mrs. Dunley, the school nurse and general badass in chaos; and Principal Lewis. "Quick as you can," I added when her eyes widened. Meanwhile, I focused on securing the scissors, calming Polly, and ensuring Jamie wasn't holding anything else sharp. Steps, clear and steady, that's what I knew to do.

If a teacher suspected a child had been harmed, the steps were clear: document everything, speak to the designated safeguarding lead—in this case, Principal Lewis—and under no circumstances, ask complicated questions. Get facts, keep calm, and let the professionals handle the investigation.

"Okay," I said, forcing calm. "First things first." I crouched in front of Polly. "Pol, I know this feels awful, but I promise we'll sort this out."

Polly's hair had been woven into four neat braids down to her waist. Jamie had sliced through one of them halfway up, leaving a ragged stump where the braid used to fall. Polly shoved Jamie, her face twisting with fury. "I hate you!" she screamed. "My princess hair!" she wailed.

Jamie stumbled back, still crying, eyes wide. As

he moved, his sleeve shifted, revealing dark bruises along his forearm—deep, purple blotches that stood out starkly against his pale skin. My breath hitched, but I forced myself to stay calm as he scurried under the play table, clutching a teddy bear, sobbing as loudly as Polly.

Okay. Every step of this had to be recorded, and I knew I'd be writing a detailed report by the end of the day. The bruises on Jamie's arm couldn't be ignored. What the hell was I supposed to do now? Polly's hair was ruined, Jamie was sobbing under the table, and those bruises on Jamie... those bruises. My mind raced, cataloging what I'd seen, what I needed to ask, and what I'd need to report. This wasn't just a school incident anymore. Something bigger was happening here. Focus, Finn. One step at a time.

I turned to Polly -- her face still blotchy and red, her breath in stuttering gasps. I wiped her damp cheeks gently with the edge of my sleeve. "Polly," I said softly. "You're still you, and you're still beautiful. Okay? Your hair doesn't change that." I paused, waiting for her to look at me.

She sobbed harder, barely taking a breath in that way kids do when they're inconsolable.

"Breathe with me," I tried. "In for four... "

Nothing. Polly just shook her head violently. I had

to think fast. Thankfully, Mrs. Dunley appeared, striding in with the calm authority that always seemed to follow her. She looked at Polly, red-faced and hiccupping, then at Jamie curled under the table, knowing this wasn't just a minor playground spat. Our eyes met, and in that brief exchange, I knew she understood the urgency. Without a word, she knelt beside Polly, murmuring gentle reassurances while I moved toward Jamie, who was still sobbing into his teddy bear.

Once Polly was safe with Mrs. Dunley, and Mrs. Gilbert had taken all the other children into the playground, it was just Jamie and me. I waited momentarily until someone else stepped into the classroom. Principal Lewis hovered just out of our vision, clipboard in hand. Seeing her there stiffened my shoulders. I hated that I couldn't console Jamie without a witness, but whatever those bruises meant, this was serious. Jamie was curled into himself, still clutching the teddy bear, his shoulders shaking. I knelt slowly, close enough that he could feel my presence without feeling cornered.

"Jamie," I said softly. "It's okay."

He buried his face in the bear, still crying, and I gently eased up his sleeve to get a better look at the bruises—fingertip bruises. "Can you tell me what happened today?"

His chin lifted. "My hair isn't girly!" he repeated defiantly. "Mom said... but Dad... " He sobbed again, and after exchanging a glance with Principal Lewis, I went under the table and tugged him onto my lap. He immediately buried himself in my chest, his thin frame shaking with every breath. With my free hand, I pulled out my phone and took photos of the bruises for evidence in case Jamie wasn't ready to talk yet.

NINE

Walker
_____

IF I WERE A SKIPPING SORT OF MAN, I WOULD HAVE
been capering into the community center.

Instead of prancing from my truck—as in I had
driven myself to my art class, praise all the gods of
independence—I walked along enjoying the several
inches of snow piled beside the salted walk. I was
going for nonchalance on the outside, while inside I
was stupid-excited.

Not only was tonight the night I was going to give
Finn his gift, re-wrapped neatly, but I was going to
ask him out on a date. An official one. With no other
jeering lemurs making fart jokes or starting sing-a-
longs in the donut shop. Seriously, who other than
Arnaud in our little messed-up group knew the lyrics

to "Petit Papa Noël"? No one. Not even the donut maker Jean Claude.

My plans for tonight were to arrive early, gift Finn his statuette, and then, ask him out. Also, I was going to pass along the news that I was officially cleared to restart my life. Driving, obviously, but also hockey. Dr. Quackers had signed off on my returning to play, as well as being behind the wheel. The side effects of the meds had lessened dramatically over time. The good effects were still there, and I felt much more like a functional human being instead of a roided-out rabid gorilla.

Bubbling with excitement, I jogged into the center, down the hall, and exploded into the art room, expecting to find Finn setting up and looking super cute in a silly Christmas sweater. We'd all agreed to wear one. Since I had not previously engaged in holiday mirth, I had to order one online. The things a person did to fit in with his peers. You'd think once you graduated high school that shit would stop, but nope. Humans were weird.

"Bonjour! I, too, have come early. I brought some homemade maple fudge just like my Maman makes." I gaped at Arnaud, clad in a hideous sweater with little silver bells that jingled with each of his expressive arm waves. "We are setting up for treats since the donut shop closes early for a rented party. Come in, mon ami, and help us make the punch!" Finn stood behind the desk, smiling softly as he dumped ginger ale into a punch bowl. "It will be no alcohol as we are all recovering from our own mental things, plus taking the meds for happy brains. But do not fear. It will be magnifique, for it has a secret ingredient only my family knows of. Come, Walker, help us make ready!"

I seriously wanted to slap him for being here. Fuck his fudge. I had something to give to Finn. Now I'd have to wait until all the chuckleheads left after class.

"Why are you like this?" I asked the bubbly goalie. He merely shrugged before digging into a cloth grocery sack for some oranges.

"I am just a lucky, happy man," he replied, then returned to his fruit, a knife coming from within the bag with a flourish that he also was known to display when catching pucks. "So, you can come work with us. Maybe you will catch my good mood, non?"

"No," I mumbled and removed my coat. Finn's eyes widened when he saw my candy cane sweater. His was cute. Just little pine trees. Not ugly at all. "Not one word," I told the two punch makers. They both bit back sniggers. I found nothing humorous at all and held onto my grumpy mood until I was nudging the jokers out the door after class with their dumb little oils of themselves as holiday cookies. Cookies. How did Finn come up with these ideas? What kind of cookie would you be? I'd been tempted to paint a turd cookie, but didn't want to disappoint Finn, so I painted a ginger cookie because I was spicy and had a dabble of Swedish blood on my mother's side.

When Chip bumbled out the door with a mouthful of fudge, I closed it behind him, then turned to look at Finn.

"Are you okay tonight? You seem a little agitated," he asked as he stood by an empty easel, brows tangled in concern.

"I'm good. Honestly, I just… " I took a second to center and breathe. Dr. Quackers would be tugging his goatee in glee if he could see me putting his calming suggestions into play. "I'm just a little edgy because I had plans for tonight and they kind of went south. That made me feel anxious and out of control. But, and this is a big but, I'm seeing my reaction for what it is and am working through it now."

"Wow, you sure have picked up that counseling jargon. Good on you."

I would have risen up onto my toes at the praise,

but I wasn't ten. "Yeah, well, it's kind of been inserted into my brain over the past few months. Emotional responses to triggers, underlying issues, yadda yadda." I shrugged it all off. I didn't want Finn to see me as weak. "So, I got you something."

He blinked. "I didn't get you anything. I thought we were just doing the party and—"

"No, hey, no, it's cool. Seriously." I hurried over to him, close enough to smell his cologne but not be too intimidating. Man, Dr. Quackers would blow a psychiatric nut when I told him about tonight. "I don't really want anything. Holidays are tense for me. I kind of... well, I'm working on all of that, so please don't feel obligated. I just wanted to give you something that showed how much this class has meant to me." He seemed unable to speak and just nodded. I dashed to my coat, ran back, and held out the clumsily wrapped present. "I'm not really good at wrapping gifts. Never had much practice, so if you don't want to open it, then—"

He shook his head softly as his eyes grew dewy. "I think you did a fine job." He tore into the paper like a Schnauzer sniffing out a new dog bone under the fancy blue and white wrap. I had to chuckle. He stared at the little ceramic teacher for so long that I was beginning to feel uncomfortable. Did he hate it? Was it a dumb gift for an adult to give another adult? Shit. It was dumb. I knew it.

"This is so sweet, thank you." He turned those wet hazel eyes to me, and I felt something incredibly strong well up inside my chest. "It's just so thoughtful… "

"Well, you've been really patient with me. I know I'm an asshole."

"No. You are *not* an asshole. You're a tender man with a very strong suit of armor."

That made me laugh out loud. "Oh yeah, that's me. Sir Walker, Knight of the Copperheads, slayer of net crashers, hero of Rochester." We both snickered. "I saw it, and it was so you. I know it's probably something a kid would give you, but I'm not good at shopping and, well, yeah."

"It's lovely. I will cherish it always."

That made me feel light as a snow cloud. "Cool. So, uhm, I know I'm not exactly the finest catch in the sea, but if you were okay with it, I thought maybe we could go out sometime?" A tiny twitch at the corner of his lips confused me. "Or not. I mean if there's some sort of thing where a teacher shouldn't date a student. Oh. Well, okay, obviously teachers shouldn't date underage kids, but I'm not sure about that line when it's two grown men and—"

"Walker, there is no wrong or right gift. If it's from the heart, then it's the right gift."

I nodded dully. His gaze held mine. "I would really like to kiss you, but you haven't said yes or no to a date. I don't want to kiss a dude who isn't into going out with me."

"Sorry. I am feeling all the feels right now. I would very much like to go out with you sometime."

"Cool. Okay, cool." I blew out a long exhalation. "So, I guess we should maybe wait until after this class ends in a few more weeks just to like ensure I'm back on my life track and no one can fault you for doing something morally gray."

"That sounds wonderful. Our ten-week class is over in two weeks."

"Yeah, good. And I'll be back on the ice by then, so I'll have to check my schedule, but for sure, I want to take you out for dinner."

He rose onto his toes to kiss me gently on the cheek. Soft as a kitten's whiskers, and just as ticklish. His lips lingered on my scruffy cheek for a few moments. It took every ounce of willpower I had not to turn my face or hug him to me. When he lowered back to his feet, I gazed at him with a doofy smile. He returned my dorky smile with one of his own.

"Guess we should clean up and head home," he offered, and I bobbed my head.

I toted all the easels out for him, tucked them into his car, and then took his hand in mine to press a kiss to his cold knuckles.

"See you next class," I whispered, then dropped his hand. He patted my face before driving off. I looked around, saw the area was empty, and skipped back to my truck.

THE FOLLOWING NIGHT, I WAS ON THE ICE. IN A game. Ya-freaking-hoo.

Instead of listening to a lovely young lady singing the anthem, I was being barraged by a rather upset goalie.

"I do not understand why you do not tell the rest of us about the statue. It is not such a thing as being big or not small, no, it is that we would have liked to maybe chirp in."

I shot Arnaud a glower as we stood in a tidy line in front of the bench. I'd never guessed that Finn would share a picture of my gift on his Instagram account or that the other guys in art class followed him. I mean, yeah, I did, but that was because I was a sappy shit who liked to look at the images of him doing fun things while looking super adorable. Masturbation may have been involved as well while scrolling, but I was a guy with an active libido. Sue me.

"Chip," I growled over my shoulder as the singer reached a high note that made the entire bench wince.

"Yeah?" Chip asked, craning his head to look back at me.

"No, not you. I was telling Arnie that the term is chip in not chirp in," I explained. Coach gave me a dark look. I shut up. Chip nodded. Seemed he didn't care. Nor did Bob or Taft. Only our emotional second-string goalie was upset.

Chip nodded like he didn't care, but then, as usual, he couldn't help himself. "Actually, 'chip in' comes from poker," he said, twisting slightly on the bench to face me. "Early 1800s. Everyone had to put a chip into the pot to be part of the hand. So it just sort of morphed into meaning contributing to anything: money, ideas, effort."

Arnaud rolled his eyes. "Chirp, chip, chap. It is all for the good you know what I am meaning. I am not angry. No, no, I am hurt. I wish for next time, when we do art classes, we will present Teacher Finn with a gift from us all. This way, emotions are happy and not flat. Oui?"

"Yes, oui, sure, da, ja, whatever." Oh my God. I wasn't sure which tendie was worse. The Russian who called people otters and broke his stick in half when he missed a save, or the French Canadian who talked incessantly while trying to make friends with the ice. Goaltenders were a whole different breed. "Fine, we'll all chip in to buy Finn something. Can we maybe play hockey now?"

"Oui. We can play. Thank you for consideration of my feelings. You are not always un gros canard."

"Thanks?" He clapped my shoulder and sat back down in his backup goalie chair. I dropped onto my ass on the bench, eager for the third line to roll. I was ready. More than ready. I was stoked. This was the way back to Manhattan. Getting to play, proving I was a new man, letting the GM back in New York eyeball me being a good noodle.

I shot Bob a look as we hit the ice. He and I had been paired up, a blessing because I knew him from art class, and the other D-men seemed to be kind of wary of me. Like they didn't trust me not to clock them for some minor infraction. Which, given I had punched one of the Vipers in the face a year ago for some stupid practical joke, was a legit concern. The road back to the pros was a long, long, long, long one to walk. I saw many foot blisters in my future.

"You ready to knock heads and chew gum?" Bob asked as we skated out to join in a breakaway in the making. I saw Taft lose the puck, a nasty turnover, and got the puck carrier for Jersey locked into my sights. My check to his shoulder was clean but hard. It knocked him into the boards, leaving the puck sitting there like a cupcake for a good boy. I did love cupcakes. I shoveled it up, chugged down the ice to the Jersey net, and fired. It bounced off the upright with a clang. The Copperhead fans all AWWW'd at the same time. I skated behind the net, eyes on the puck, and entered a nice little knot of players in the corner. Elbows were higher than they should be as we all poked at the little frozen rubber disc down by our skates. When one such elbow connected with my eye, I did not react. Left eye watering, I kicked the puck free and grinned at the Jersey player as a whistle blew.

My smile followed Elbow Boy all the way to the sin bin. We didn't score on the power play, but I did pull a penalty, which made me and our defensive coach happy. Blood pumping through my veins, sweat in my sore eye, I felt about as good as a man could feel.

Win or lose, my life was back on track. Now all it needed for a cherry topper was a dinner date and a goodnight kiss from the world's best teacher.

TEN

Finn
———

It was the last of the ten mandated art lessons with my hockey guys, and I was surprised by how sad I felt that it was ending. What had started as an awkward, reluctant series of sessions had grown into something I looked forward to. Sure, I'd have more time for my thesis now, but I would miss the weekly meetings, the easy laughter, the chaotic energy, and the unexpected friendships. With their jokes and teasing, these guys had become more than just students in my class—they felt like my people.

Even two weeks after Christmas, the room smelled faintly of pine from the garland someone had stubbornly refused to take down. But the thick snow and the freezing temperatures had inspired today's project, winter landscapes, and an attempt at mastering impasto painting, thick layers of oil paint sculpted with palette knives to create texture. Taft had gone wild, slathering bold streaks of icy blue and snowy white across his canvas in chaotic swipes. Bob was more careful, painting in deliberate strokes of slate gray and shadowy blacks that captured the starkness of frozen branches against a cold sky. Walker had made something softer, blurry trees fading into snowfall. Arnaud and Chip had both gone to create a frozen lake.

The conversation turned nostalgic, and they shared childhood memories of pond skating as kids.

Arnaud spoke fondly of his winters in Quebec, where the icy ponds and lakes sounded like a part of daily life. His voice grew tight when he talked about his father teaching him to skate and how they'd race across the frozen surface while his dad laughed and shouted support.

"I wish he still… " he began, coughing lightly. He forced a smile and changed the subject before the emotion could overwhelm him. "What about you, Chip?"

"Every winter, my brothers and I built bonfires on the shore of the lake. We'd pile up driftwood, get it roaring, warm our hands until they stung, then skate until the stars came out. It should've felt like magic.

And maybe it did, for them. But all I could think about was how fast a fire spreads. Did you know a house fire can double in size every thirty seconds? And it only takes about three minutes for a room to be fully engulfed."

No one quite knew what to say to that.

Bob leaned back in his chair, arms crossed loosely, voice low and a little gravelly. "Back home in Minnesota, my dad used to test the ice before we were allowed on it. He'd grab this big-ass branch—like, heavy enough to swing like a bat—and just slam it down on the ice a few times." He paused, a hint of a smile tugging at the corner of his mouth. "Said if the ice didn't crack under that, it could handle a couple of dumb kids with skates. We'd be bouncing up and down behind him, dying to get on, but he always made us wait."

He looked down at his hands, thumb running over a scar on his knuckle. "Never let us take chances. Said the lake doesn't care how old you are or if you think you're tough. You fall through, then you fall through."

There was a silence after that profound statement from the big man, a stillness that hung for just a moment before someone cleared their throat.

Taft fidgeted in his chair. "I was only three the

first time I skated on the pond. My best friend swore up and down it was safe, but I kept freaking out because I could hear the ice creaking. With every step, a horrible cracking sound." He mimicked the noise dramatically, drawing snorts from Bob. "Anyway," Taft continued, his smile faltering just a little. "I got maybe six feet before I panicked, fell straight on my ass, and somehow managed to drag Mick down with me. We both slid halfway across the pond like two sacks of potatoes."

He chuckled softly, then looked down at his hands, his voice hitching. "There aren't enough good things to remember."

"What about you?" Bob asked Walker, but he showed every sign he didn't want to talk about the pond because he immediately changed the subject.

"Present time!" he announced. Bob then left the room and came back with a big box wrapped in shiny red paper, topped with a crooked bow. Scrawled on the side in bold scarlet marker was the word TEACH. Given his love of anything red and dramatic, I assumed this was Taft's handiwork. "Open it," Walker urged.

I tugged at the paper and pulled out a Copperhead hoodie.

"That's Walker's number," Chip announced as I

traced his last name, HANNAN, and the number 10. "You know, only about 8 percent of defensemen in pro hockey wear the number 10 on their jersey. It's usually a forward's number, so when a defenseman picks it, it usually means one of two things: they're honoring someone, or they just really don't care about position-number conventions. Statistically, number 10 defensemen block more shots than average. Like, significantly more. It's like they've got something to prove." He subsided. "Sorry."

"Why 10 then, Walker?" I asked.

He shrugged, like it didn't matter. "Because it used to be this kid Julian's number. Back on my junior team. Cocky bastard wouldn't shut up about it and said no one else could wear it after he got drafted."

Walker looked off into the middle distance, jaw tight. "So, when I signed with my first pro team and saw 10 was free, I grabbed it. Just to be petty. No deep meaning. No childhood hero. I just wanted him to see it on the stat sheets and know I was still here even if he fucked it all up and ended up an accountant." He gave a sharp exhale that might've been a laugh. "Stupid, really. But I kept it."

I nodded in encouragement and then met Walker's

gaze. He stared back at me, and we smiled at each other.

Before I could even react, Bob elbowed him hard in the ribs, earning a grunt. Arnaud, perched on the other side of Walker, sniggered and jabbed him with his elbow from the opposite direction.

"Ah, quelqu'un a le feu pour le professeur," Arnaud teased, his French accent curling the words. "Someone 'as it 'ot for teacher."

Walker flushed a deep red, scowling at Arnaud while Taft outright cackled from across the room. I couldn't help but smile—part amused, part... something else. The blush crept up Walker's neck, and the way he ducked his head, looking both embarrassed and oddly pleased, was adorable. Something warm unfurled in my chest, and I knew I was in trouble.

Beneath the hoodie was a bag of my favorite coffee from the little shop across the road, the one I always joked about being the only thing strong enough to keep me functioning. I smiled at that, already picturing my first cup.

There was an envelope as well, and when I opened it, two glossy season tickets slid out. Copperheads season tickets. "By the glass," Walker explained, his voice softer as he waited for my reaction.

Chip leaned forward. "You know, they didn't always use the kind of plexiglass we have now. Back in the '70s and '80s, it was acrylic and rigid as hell. Didn't flex much on impact. Players would hit it at full speed and just bounce off like rag dolls. Concussions, shoulder injuries… it was basically like hitting a wall." He tapped his temple. "Nowadays, it's polycarbonate. Still strong, but it has give. Absorbs impact better. Statistically, there's been a 17 percent drop in glass-related injuries since the switch. Seventeen. That's a lot of spared collarbones. And in 1987, they—"

"Jesus, Chip, enough with the stats!" Bob snapped, and Chip paled and dipped his head.

"Sorry, I just… sorry."

Bob groaned. "No. Shit, I'm sorry," Bob said and tapped his head. "My bad. That was interesting about the glass," he added, and then it was his turn to look embarrassed.

Walker pulled the subject back to the tickets. "So, you and a friend can be right up there watching us… if you want."

"My brother's a huge hockey fan, so he can explain it all to me," I said, my voice catching just a little. I glanced around at them, my chest tightening with something warm and unfamiliar. I'd grown used to end-of-year gifts: boxes of chocolates, hand-drawn macaroni art projects, and maybe the occasional friendship bracelet. But this... this was something else. "You didn't have to do this."

"We wanted to," Taft said with a shrug. "And anyway... " He grinned wickedly. "There's more under the cardboard." He pointed at the box.

I pushed the corrugated cardboard aside and nestled carefully in crisp white tissue paper was a set of paints, Bagni Venezia Pigmenti, handmade in a small village in Tuscany. The jars were weighty in my hands, and the pigments inside were like liquid jewels: deep sapphire blue, rich crimson, and buttery ochre. They shimmered under the light, each one more stunning than the last. Next to them was a set of sleek, wooden-handled brushes, each with delicate bristles that looked almost too fine.

"Fuck," I muttered and, then, glanced up with an apology on the tip of my tongue.

"Don't say it's inappropriate," Walker said before I could even begin to explain how moved I was and, yeah, how it wasn't needed.

The rest nodded.

"Tell him… " Bob said and nudged Chip who was wide-eyed.

"Really?"

"You're dying to tell him," Bob encouraged.

"But I don't have to, I know not everyone—"

"Tell him," the other three players chorused, with Walker gesturing for him to carry on as well.

"Well, uhm… " He clenched and unclenched his fingers. "Bagni Venezia Pigmenti only produces 312 pans of watercolor a year. Handmade, sun-dried, and mulled on marble slabs in a village with a population of 187. They use lake pigments from iron-rich clay deposits that haven't been commercially mined since the 1600s. Their Ultramarine Light has a particle grind variance of less than 2 microns. There's a three-year waitlist for their Sap Green and one tube of their discontinued Terra di Notte sold for nearly seven hundred euros last year." He sat back then as if he could relax now he'd told us what he knew.

"Okay. Let's meet up after this is all done, maybe every few weeks, okay? Not to paint, but to… get coffee… "

There was a chorus of agreement.

We planned a date to meet up, and then, one by one, my new friends left, until finally, it was just

Walker and me. He walked me to my car, helped me get everything inside, and then waited.

"About *our* date?" he asked, his voice hesitant. "Do you still want to—"

"Yes." The word shot out faster than I meant, and my heart stuttered. "I mean… sure." Did I sound too eager? Probably. My stomach twisted with that familiar knot of nerves tightening. Why was I so nervous?

"I'll probably fuck it up," Walker muttered, half under his breath, stuffing his hands in his pockets.

"Me too," I admitted. "But… I'm still looking forward to it."

"How could you fuck it up?" he asked, trying to sound casual, but his voice caught halfway. "You're like… effortless."

I snorted. "Yeah, right. I'm awkward as hell, and I overthink everything."

"Same," he said, smiling.

"Guess we're both doomed then."

"Next Friday? I could pick you up—"

"Yes." The word jumped out before I could temper it, and heat flooded my face. Too eager, too desperate, too… me. My chest felt tight. What if I said something stupid? What if I read too much into this?

Walker didn't seem to notice my inner meltdown. He reached out, fingers warm against my cheek, his touch light but sure. "I can't wait," he said softly. "Can I... "

Kiss me? Fuck yes. His lips brushed mine, soft at first, just the faintest press of warmth against warmth. I thought that might be it—a fleeting kiss, nothing more—but then Walker shifted closer, his fingers sliding along my jaw as he tilted his head and deepened it. Slow, deliberate, and wow, my heart stumbled over itself. His lips parted just slightly, inviting me to follow, and I did. My hands found his jacket as if I needed something solid to cling to, and when he finally pulled back, my breath was shaky and uneven. "Wow," I said, a little dazed.

"Yeah," Walker whispered, his thumb brushing along my cheekbone. "Me too."

He lingered a beat longer than I expected, his fingers curling slightly against my skin. His gaze dropped to my mouth, then back to my eyes, and for a moment, I thought he might kiss me again. My heart pounded, and everything inside me screamed, *stay, stay*. But instead, Walker exhaled softly, stepping back with an awkward smile. "We should exchange numbers," he said. "I'll figure out what we're doing. And really... you should go now."

I wasn't sure I wanted to go. My car keys felt heavier in my hand than they should, like leaving now meant I might wake up tomorrow and wonder if any of this had really happened. But it was right to leave —give him space, give me time to breathe. I nodded. "Okay. See you Friday."

"Yeah," Walker said again, softer this time, and I swear his smile followed me all the way home.

———

THE SCHOOL WEEK WAS SLOW AND FRAUGHT WITH worries about Jamie and his family. So many meetings and endless discussions never seemed to lead anywhere. When a school suspects a child is experiencing issues at home that may be causing harm to them, they typically follow a structured procedure. One we're all too familiar with, but one that deeply hurts every teacher's heart.

Paperwork piled up, and incident reports and behavior logs filled folders thicker than textbooks. Then there was the waiting—hoping the system would move quickly enough—that the right people would step in before things got worse. It was a process designed to protect children, but it left teachers feeling helpless, forced to stand on the sidelines when they wanted to reach out and fix things themselves.

At the center of it all was a confused six-year-old Jamie. His dad had moved out, and notes on every file warned staff that he would be refused access if he showed up at the school. Jamie's world was unraveling, and we were all scrambling to hold the pieces together.

Every morning, I scanned the playground, looking for him. Yesterday, I spotted him standing off to one side, head down, watching the other kids as if they were moving into another world. One he no longer knew how to enter. On the worst days, he wouldn't meet my eyes at all.

I wanted to help, but what could I do? I couldn't follow him home. I couldn't be there when the quiet turned to chaos or when the silence became unbearable. All I could do was offer him calm in my classroom—a quiet smile, a few extra minutes to finish his work, a whispered "Good job"—that I hoped made him feel seen. It never felt like enough.

Polly had forgiven Jamie for cutting her hair faster than anyone expected. She'd barely blinked when the principal had explained what happened, shrugging it off with a quick, "It'll grow back." But that was Polly—fiercely loyal in a way most six-year-olds hadn't figured out yet. Since then, she has been wandering around the playground with Jamie, her small hand tucked protectively in his. She kept him talking, chattering about cartoons, her cat, and the new shoes she insisted made her run faster. Sometimes Jamie didn't say much in return, but he seemed to like having her there.

It was finally Friday, and the only bright light on an otherwise bleak school week was the thought of my date with Walker. Admittedly, I'd spent an embarrassing amount of time deciding what to wear. I wanted to appear as if I wasn't trying too hard but still cared. Too formal, and I'd look ridiculous. Too casual, and I'd regret it. He assured me the restaurant he was taking me to wasn't formal. Eventually, I settled on my favorite pair of dark jeans and a fitted sweater that somehow made my shoulders look broader than they were. It felt like a balance, and I hoped it was right when I laid everything on my bed, ready to change.

Now, I just needed to get home, shower, change, and focus on the bright spot ahead—my date with Walker. However, when I reached the parking lot, someone was leaning on my car. Jamie's dad. I stopped cold, my heart thudding in my chest. The parking lot was empty now. The kids had all gone home, and it was just the two of us. He was slouched against the driver's side door, arms crossed, his expression dark. Something about how he was waiting—too still, too laidback—set my nerves on edge, and I pulled out my cell phone.

He held his hands outward, palms up, flashing a smile that didn't quite reach his eyes. "Sorry to bother you," he said, his voice smooth, almost too calm. He extended his hand, but I didn't shake it. My mind raced, cycling through every possible outcome. Was he here to argue? To threaten me? My overactive imagination had me pinning the asshole to the ground. With my keys gripped tight in my hand just in case things escalated, I shifted my weight, standing taller, trying to project confidence I wasn't sure I felt.

"I was just wondering how Jamie's getting on." He was trying for genuine concern, but something about it felt off as if he was performing kindness rather than feeling it.

"I'm sorry," I said, keeping my voice firm. "But any questions you have should go through Principal Lewis."

Something flickered behind his smile for a moment, sharp and unmistakable resentment. Then, it was replaced by a grin that felt even more slimy than his fake concern.

"Of course," he said, voice syrupy and slow. "Of course."

He straightened then, but instead of leaving right away, he took a slow step toward me, his gaze narrowing. My pulse kicked up, and I instinctively shifted back a step. It was way too quiet now, just the faint hum of distant traffic and the cold bite of January air pressing in.

I looked at the school's security cameras, their dull red lights blinking steadily above us. He followed my gaze, lips curling into something that wasn't quite a smile.

"Mr. Carter," he said, his voice lower now, like he wanted me to know this wasn't over. He turned on his heel, walking away with a slow, deliberate swagger that made my skin crawl.

I ran back into the school, logged what I considered an intimidating incident, and then, copied an email to the principal, other teachers, and all official channels, including the cops. Maybe I was overreacting, but when the welfare of one of my students was at stake, nothing was too much.

I couldn't shake the feeling that Jamie's dad would be back, and this wasn't over. The knot in my stomach lingered long after I drove away, my mind running endless scenarios of what might happen next.

Would he show up again? Would he corner Jamie outside school or try something worse? What would I tell him if he showed up again? I imagined confrontations, arguments, and threats, and each scenario ended the same: how would I keep Jamie safe?

Then, I thought about whether I'd stay calm and try to reason with him. Or would I snap and let the anger I felt boil over? And what if it turned physical? Would I be fast enough? Strong enough? I hated how powerless I felt, like no matter how much I tried to prepare, I wouldn't be enough.

By the time I reached my driveway, I felt mentally exhausted. My mind tried to hold on to the bad, to let the worry fester, but then my thoughts shifted. Walker. The date. Something good to hold onto. Something better.

I'd done everything I could. Although I hated the situation and wanted to do more, I had to let it go for now. Until Monday, all I could do was focus on what was ahead.

And right then, what was ahead was something worth being happy about.

I wished I could find my freaking smile.

ELEVEN

Walker

_____

"OH, MY FREAKING GOD, WALKER, *MOVE OVER*!"

Harper drove an elbow into my side that Gordie Howe would have loved. I grunted but stood my ground. There was only one mirror. She was going to have to share. "Why are you even in here? Since when do you spend ten minutes trimming your nose hair?"

"Okay, first thing. I am not trimming my nose hair. I'm just making sure none are sticking out." I tipped my head back. She made a yucky face, then used her ass to push me behind her.

"That is so gross. Why are you worried about your nose hairs? You said you were meeting the art guys for pizza and a movie," she grumbled as she began applying eyeliner to her left lid. I reached up to rub my nose. "Dude! Do not bump me. Holy hell! Why are you so big and dopey?"

"This is a community space."

"Like hell. Get out. Go pluck your nasty body hairs in private."

Knowing I was likely to get a roundhouse kick to the mug, I shuffled out of the cramped bathroom. The door hit me on the ass on the way out.

"Chicks are so emotional," I whispered through the door. Profanities that would make my teammates blush flowed through the crack of the door. Snickering softly, I padded back to my bedroom. And that was when I hit problem number one. What to wear. This was a special night. Finally, Finn and I were able to go out together. That kiss we shared had lingered in my head. I'd even gotten sideswiped by Bob in morning skate during a scrimmage. Like totally laid out on my ass with a body check that really wasn't all that robust. I'd just been daydreaming along the boards instead of paying attention to the locomotive named O'Ryan chugging down the tracks at me. The other Copperheads found it humorous as hell. Even Coach smiled. Bob patted my helmet and offered me a hand as I sat on the ice.

"Better get your head in the game, Han-Man."

Rubbing my ass as I stood, I chuckled and nodded. It was kind of nice to have a nickname. That was a rather big sign of acceptance in hockey. Not that I would have chosen Han-Man, but The Great One was already taken, so Han-Man it was.

I pulled open my closet and folded my arms over my bare chest. There was really nothing that stood out in my wardrobe. Most of my suits hung there, covered with dry cleaner plastic, having not been worn since I'd been in Rochester. The pros had a strict dress code, citing that suits had to be worn to games. This league was a little more lax. The Copperheads did ask that we dress respectably, with no offensive slogans on our clothing. I usually just pulled on some clean jeans, a tee, and a Copperhead hoodie. Maybe a toque in our team colors of cream, black, and gold. Some nice sneakers. Done.

But this was not a hoodie and jeans night. I wanted to look good, impress Finn, and show him that even though I was a hockey player with some head issues, I could romance a man with class. The eatery I had chosen wasn't too fancy, but it wasn't flip-flops and torn shorts either. Not that anyone was wearing flip-flops as the temps were hovering around zero. Aside from Arnaud, but I suspected he wore them just to try to prove how much tougher Canadians were than the American players. I'd caught him soaking his cold toes in a hot foot bath before gearing up for last night's game, but I kept that tidbit to myself for future use.

I began rooting through my clothes. Fifteen minutes later, I had five outfits tossed over my unmade bed. I hated all five.

With a sigh, I exited my room and crossed the hall to rap on Harper's door. She called me in, so I stepped into her domain. She was on the bed in a baggy sleep shirt, legs in a lotus, and hair pulled up atop her head in some sort of wild do. Her gaze flitted from the bottle of nail polish in her hand to me. Three toes on her left foot were painted crimson.

"I'm painting," she told me as if I couldn't see that.

"Can I get your thoughts on what to wear?" I asked and instantly knew I should have just pulled on whatever. Her slim brows narrowed, a small hoop in her right brow catching the light from a garage sale lava lamp beside her bed. She was watching season one of some anime about a kid and his demon protector. Typical Harper show.

"Why are you worried about clothes to meet the guys for pizza?"

"Never mind." I spun and left. I heard her feet hit the floor.

"Wait, just wait." I walked faster. She thumped into my room behind me, walking with toes up and heel down on one foot but normal on the other. "This is... shit, this is a mess. Okay, so this chaos," she waved her red nail polish bottle at the heap of shirts and pants on the bed, "tells me that you are *not* having pizza with the art guys."

"How did we even get that name?" I asked as I reached for a striped polo. She pulled it out of my hand.

"Do not ever wear that out in public. Are you going on a date?"

I thought to lie. I really did, but I could never deceive Harper. We'd been through too much together.

"I'm meeting Finn for dinner."

Her brown eyes, the same deep cocoa shade as mine, went wide. She squealed at top volume, then did a funky little dance. I rolled my eyes and folded my arms.

"Yes! I knew it. I knew you liked him! I could tell by how you talked about him. I insist on meeting him soon!" She gave me a fast hug, passed over her bottle of red polish, and started flinging clothes about the room. "Nope, no, oh God, this has stains. Nope, ugly, super old." Shirts and pants were tossed over her shoulder with wild abandon.

"I'll just wear a suit," I said, and got a dark glower over her shoulder.

"No, a suit is too stiff. I think we can use some dress slacks and dress them down." She started shoving clothes into my chest. Dark gray slacks, a light blue dress shirt, and a smoky ash sweater. "Do them. Oh, and a watch. Do you have boots?"

"Uhm, maybe? Like hiking boots?" I shuffled the clothes in my arms.

"Well, yeah, if nothing else. Are they black? Let me see." She dove into my closet, emerging a few minutes later with black suede shoes I'd forgotten I owned, a sleek belt, and a coat that would keep me warm for about five seconds. "This is what you wear. The coat is for looks only, so don't plan to be outside for too long. Dress socks. Do *not* pull on some ugly old tube socks that you've jerked off into. Right. Get dressed. I'm going to call the girls from the gym and tell them I'm running late to get to the club. I love that you're dating!"

She gave me a quick hug and then ran off, leaving me standing in a pair of fleece joggers with an armful of date attire, chuckling.

Five minutes later, I was dressed. I had to admit my sister knew how to clothe a man for a night out with his art teacher slash hopeful steady dating guy. Man, that was a long title.

"Take it one step at a time, Walker," I whispered to myself before heading out to meet the man I had pulled on too-tight boots for.

CHRYSANTHOS' CAFÉ WAS PACKED. I WAS REALLY glad I had reserved a table because the tiny club was wall-to-wall diners. Stepping out of the cold, I waited as instructed by a sign telling me the hostess would seat me. I removed my coat and hung it up on the coat rack to my left.

My nerves were on edge. Glancing into the dining area, I saw that most of the tables were occupied by couples. This was a really nice place to go on a date —small but trendy—with a three-piece band of older men seated on a triangular stage in the far corner, playing a lyra, a bouzouki, and a small drum, performing soft Greek tavern songs. The lights were low, the music mellow, and the aromas of veal stew, the special tonight, filled the warm air. A blast of cold air blew in behind me. I turned to see Finn hustling inside, his hair coated with soft flakes, his cheeks bright pink.

"Hey," I said as he skidded to a halt just inside the door.

"Wow," he replied, his eyes moving over me from head to toe. "You look incredible."

He shrugged out of his coat with my help. I gave him a quick head-to-toe. "I clean up okay. So do you. Look incredible, I mean. Really sexy," I replied and found a hanger for his winter coat. His outfit was much like mine. Slacks, a sweater over a shirt, and a dark green scarf that made his hazel eyes pop. I wanted to tell him I thought he was pretty, but that seemed a private thing. "My sister picked out my clothes."

Thankfully, the hostess, a lovely young woman with long black hair and olive skin, appeared with two menus and a gracious smile. A true savior, she was, because Finn must have thought I was an untrained ape who couldn't match pants with tops. That was kind of true, but still, I didn't need to broadcast my lack of style. She led us to a round table beside a window that looked out onto a snowy veranda. Little blue fairy lights outside turned the snow a soft sapphire. I hurried to pull out a seat for Finn, who blushed prettily before taking his seat.

"The waiter will be over shortly. Kali oreksi," she said before moving off.

"I hope you enjoy Greek food," I said as a waiter appeared with drink menus and a lighter to spark the wick in a slim candle in the middle of the table.

"I love it," Finn replied. We both ordered a non-alcoholic orange spritzer, then stared at each other over menus. "I really like the ambiance of this place. Also, I called my brother to ask which shirt to wear with this sweater. I was nervous."

Hearing that lessened my embarrassment. "I was nervous too. I wanted to show you that I'm not just some violent jerk."

"I know that." He reached out to touch the back of my hand. "I wouldn't have come if I didn't think you were a good man."

I may have puffed up a bit hearing that. "Thanks. I'm trying. So, how was school today?"

The warm smile he had been wearing faded. "It was a little stressful," he confessed and shook his head. "But that's not a conversation for a date. Do you want to do some appetizers? I see they have mini dolmas stuffed with lamb." I couldn't stop watching his mouth as he spoke. His lips. They were *so* pink, *so* soft. I knew what they felt like under mine, and I longed to feel those pliant—"Walker?"

"Oh, sorry, yeah, sure. Love that." He could have ordered pickled leg of brontosaurus for all I cared. "Get whatever you want. I love Greek food." He gave me a tilted little smile. Which, for some reason, engaged my damn mouth. "When we were kids, we had this old neighbor couple from Greece, Mr. and Mrs. Doukas. They lived right next door, and sometimes when things got intense, they would stand on their side porch and sing old Greek songs to let us know they were home. Harper and I would slip over when Dad was sleeping off the rage, and they would patch me up, feed us lots of moussaka and lamb meatballs, and baklava that would melt in your mouth."

He reached over the table to touch the back of my hand. I felt that gentle caress all the way to my marrow. "I'm so glad you had the Doukases to comfort you in trying times."

I nodded, uncomfortable. "That was not date talk. Sorry. I, uhm… " I looked around the busy dining area for our waiter but couldn't find him. Finn squeezed my hand before returning his attention to the menu. Relief washed through me. That was one thing I really liked about Finn. He knew I had a tractor-trailer load of bad shit in my past, but he never judged or pushed me to talk about it. He was just there, patient, kind, understanding, and willing to let me say what I wanted when I wanted. And that was why he had gotten the best teacher statuette.

"Well, I would love to try the lamb meatballs for starters. Someday, I would love to visit Greece. Have you ever been?"

"No. I've been to cold countries. The Vipers played an exhibition game in Finland last year. That was pretty cool. Got to see the Northern Lights and eat lots of fish. Like, lots of fish." That made him chuckle. "Maybe someday we can visit Greece."

And as soon as that fell out of my gob hole, I wished I could suck it back in. Sadly, there was no way I could. The comment floated by on a wave of warm air scented with the delicate aroma of braised pork a server was carrying past our table. "I mean, like on a tour or something. As friends who date." He blinked. I blew out a breath. "Okay, no, not as friends who date. As men who date. Dating men. Who kiss. And like each other. Together. To Greece. In the summer when I'm not playing and school is out. That kind of thing. But if that's too pushy, and it probably is, because I have no class when it comes to being a decent person."

"Walker, I think a trip to Greece as men who are

dating sounds wonderful. If we are still dating come summer, of course."

"Oh, nice. Well, sure, of course. I hope we are." I seriously wanted to slap myself in the face with a goalie stick. A big, fat paddle was the only thing that would do at this point. "I'm not sure why I'm being such a putz. Guys are not supposed to say how much they like someone or how they hope a new relationship works out."

He placed his menu down. The candle flickered. The hostess joined the trio in the corner to sing "I Agapi Ine Zali" for the diners. She had a really pretty voice. A few couples rose and moved to dance in front of the musicians. There wasn't much room, but nobody seemed to mind being elbow to elbow.

"I think guys should say what they feel. Right now, I'm hoping that we're still dating come summer, as well."

Feeling all kinds of things that I wasn't skilled enough to put into pretty words like Finn could, I placed my hand on the table beside the candle, palm up. He laid his smaller hand over mine, and that was when I moved from a heavy crush to falling in love, which scared me to death while it also made my toes tingle.

"Wanna dance?" I asked and got a nod. We joined

the older folks on the dance floor, the only queer couple swaying back and forth. If the others surrounding us gave us funny looks, I wouldn't have known. All I saw, once he stepped into my arms, was Finn. He eclipsed the earth and those living on it.

Yeah, I was free-falling hard and fast. I hoped the landing was a gentle one.

TWELVE

Finn

_____

THE COPPERHEADS' RINK WAS ELECTRIC TONIGHT.
Packed to capacity, the crowd was loud, enthusiastic,
and relentlessly supportive. Connor practically
vibrated with excitement beside me, leaning forward
in his seat, eyes wide, entirely absorbed by the game.
He was still in shock that my after-hours art therapy
clients had gifted me season tickets, but he didn't ask
me questions about who was in the class or why I'd
been given them.

"So they're for me?" he'd asked, confused.

"Us," I said with a grin. "I'm getting into
hockey."

"You are? Why? What changed?"

And that was where I changed the subject, and
now we were here, and we'd stopped at the

concession store to get T-shirts. I wasn't ready to wear my Walker jersey—yet. I'd bought a generic Copperheads jersey, and Connor had opted for Arnaud's jersey number because, according to him, goalies were gods.

"Did you see that save?" Connor shouted over the crowd, slapping my knee enthusiastically. "Arnaud is a freaking legend!"

"Yep," I agreed, not that I'd noticed anything beyond Walker's graceful, powerful movements across the ice. He was mesmerizing as he skated, the confidence behind every quick turn and sharp pivot. It wasn't just athletic—it was art.

"Earth to Finn," Connor teased, nudging me with his elbow. "You haven't listened to a word I've said, have you?"

I grinned sheepishly. "Sorry, hockey overload."

"Bullshit. You're watching number 10 like he's the only one out there." Connor raised an eyebrow knowingly, smirking. "Want to tell me what's *really* going on here?"

Heat rushed to my cheeks. "Nothing's going on."

"Sure. Totally believable." Connor scoffed, turning back toward the game. "I've been trying to get you interested in hockey for years. Walker Hannan shows up, and suddenly, you're a superfan?"

His eyes narrowed. "Was it him that gave you the tickets?"

"No." I wasn't lying. After all, it hadn't *just* been Walker who'd handed over the tickets. "Maybe, I finally appreciate the game," I muttered weakly, avoiding my brother's skeptical gaze.

Connor laughed, shaking his head. "Yeah, right."

On the ice, Walker moved effortlessly, his presence commanding. I found myself tracking him as he positioned himself perfectly to intercept passes, defend his goalie, and, as Connor said, "read the play" like a master strategist. I might not have fully understood all the rules yet, but I knew excellence when I saw it, and Walker was undeniably excellent.

"If he keeps playing like this, the Vipers might come calling again," Connor yelled after another shot on goal from my man.

My man.

The thought of Walker heading back to New York City made me worry. The idea of him returning to the relentless pace of the game worried me, not just because of the distance, but also because of the pressures he'd have to face there. I pushed those thoughts away quickly, choosing instead to join in the crowd's roar of approval as Walker sent another opponent crashing into the boards. For now, I wanted to enjoy these moments, these nights where Walker was right here, close enough to touch.

The Copperheads had control now, and I loved to see my art guys out on the ice. There'd been a foul or something, and Connor reliably informed me that the Copperheads were on a power play and that Walker anchored the line going over second. Chip and Taft were out there now, and they passed it one to the other, with Taft sending it speeding toward Walker. Walker caught it cleanly and skated swiftly toward the net, shoulders hunched in concentration. My breath caught, heart pounding as Walker feinted left, then snapped his stick hard, firing the puck past the goalie's outstretched glove.

"YES!" Connor jumped up beside me, pumping his fist. I rose to my feet too, clapping and cheering with the rest of the crowd. Walker's teammates swarmed him, slapping him on the helmet and shouting praise.

Amid the chaos, Walker turned, scanning the crowd until our eyes locked through the glass. A brilliant smile spread across his face, vulnerable and boyish in its pure joy. My pulse stuttered, warmth spreading through my chest as I returned the smile, my heart tripping over itself like I was fifteen and hopelessly crushing again.

Connor nudged my shoulder, breaking the connection. "Yeah, totally just here for the hockey," he teased, laughter dancing in his eyes.

"Shut up." I laughed, sinking back into my seat.

But Connor was right. I was here for Walker, for the man who skated with grace and smiled at me like I'd just given him the world. And maybe, I thought, as the game resumed, I really was becoming a hockey fan. Or at least a Walker Hannan fan, and honestly, that felt pretty amazing.

After the game, I dropped Connor at home, drove to what I called our café, and sat in the car wrapped up like a burrito in my thickest coat. Walker arrived half an hour later, still radiating excitement from the win, his eyes sparkling when he knocked on my window. Embarrassingly, I was out of the car so fast I nearly fell on my ass. Not a good start when he tugged me close to stop me from falling. We hugged and, as if I suffered from word vomit, I blurted as soon as he stood back.

"You were amazing out there," I said, unable to keep the admiration from my voice. "The way you took that puck and got a goal, and the way you did that thing with the knock from your hand and the spin, and the bit when you slid on the wall, and oh my

God, when you pushed that big guy into the boards, that was so freaking sexy."

Walker laughed softly, ducking his head modestly. "Just doing my job. Glad you enjoyed it."

"It was just... yeah... "

He gestured to the coffee shop. "Shall we?" We stepped inside together, the bell above the door chiming softly. The café was warm and scented with coffee and fresh pastries. We placed our order and then settled into our usual corner booth, comfortable and private, away from the noise and bustle of the busy counter. It felt weird that it was just the two of us. I even missed the other guys for a moment until Walker tapped my shin with his foot, and I realized how freaking awesome it was to be here alone with Walker.

He leaned back and relaxed, his smile softer and more intimate now. "If you keep coming to games, you'll know more about hockey than me."

I chuckled. "Pretty sure that's impossible. But I admit, it's grown on me."

"Only the hockey?" Walker asked, eyebrow raised and smirking.

My cheeks warmed again. "Okay. Maybe not only hockey."

He reached across the table, his fingertips

brushing lightly against mine and sending a gentle thrill through me. "I'm glad."

We talked effortlessly about everything and nothing: funny stories from my classroom, Walker's anecdotes about his teammates, and plans for the weekend. Each conversation deepened the comfortable ease between us, each laugh bringing us closer. When we left the café, the night had grown even colder, our breath fogging the air. Walker walked me to my car, pausing under the gentle glow of the streetlamp. His eyes met mine, soft, questioning, and I nodded silently, heart thumping as he leaned in to gently brush his lips against mine. A tender, lingering kiss filled with warmth and promise.

When he pulled back, his eyes searched mine, vulnerable yet hopeful. "See you soon?"

"Absolutely," I whispered, feeling like the luckiest man alive.

"I'll message you."

"I'll be waiting."

The following school week dragged by, weighed down by endless meetings and the constant worry about Jamie's situation. Every afternoon, a small knot of tension tightened in my stomach as dismissal approached, and the fear of seeing Jamie's father again lingered in my mind. The one bright spot away from all that was the messaging with Walker, stupid jokes, hockey things, and stories about the guys from the art group.

My phone buzzed, interrupting my thoughts, and I smiled when I saw Walker's name on the screen. A quick tap opened the text thread.

Walker: You will NOT believe what Arnaud did to Bob today.

Finn: Oh god, what now?

Walker: Swapped out Bob's shampoo for some glittery unicorn kid stuff. Bob didn't notice until he'd lathered it up.

I laughed, imagining Bob's reaction.

Finn: Please tell me you got pictures.

Walker: Better. Video. Bob went nuclear. Glitter everywhere.

Finn: Poor Bob. I know what glitter is like after the Christmas play. He'll be sparkling for weeks.

Walker: He's so pissed. Arnaud might be sleeping in his pads tonight.

Finn: 😂 Tell Arnaud I admire his bravery. Or insanity. Either works.

Walker: Pretty sure it's insanity.

Grinning, I set the phone down and went back to organizing art supplies and tidying up. I didn't realize how late I'd stayed but a volunteer donation of one hundred fifty sets of kid-friendly paints wasn't something I was going to leave in boxes. When I left the hallway, most teachers had already gone home. When I finally entered the empty parking lot, it was dark beyond the parking area, and I felt a cold shiver run down my spine. Just inside the glow of light was Jamie's father, leaning against my car with a tense posture and a look of simmering anger.

He straightened as I approached my car, his eyes narrowing, and I pulled out my keys and my cell in a smooth move and pressed record.

"Mr. Carter," he said, voice rough and slightly slurred. "We need to talk."

My heart pounded, but I kept my voice steady. "I'm sorry, sir, but any conversations about Jamie must happen through the principal's office."

"You think you're some hero?" he snapped and came closer. Too close. "You watch yourself, Mr. Carter. You keep out of my business, or you'll regret it. It's all Jamie can talk about, making Ella think you're gonna fix everything when there's nothing to fucking fix."

Ella? Jamie's mom, maybe?

I stood my ground, hands trembling slightly. "I'm recording this, and I'm calling 911."

"Figures." He sneered, his expression twisting bitterly.

He stumbled away, swaying as he walked backward, his gaze never leaving mine until he turned and disappeared into the growing shadows of the evening. Only when I had 911 on the line, and he was entirely out of sight, did I release a few shaky breaths that I'd been holding. I made the report, headed back into the school, filed everything -- dates, times, and what he said -- then returned to my car, locking the doors, anxiety twisting in my gut as I drove away. Now, the cops had the meeting on file, the school was aware, and Principal Lewis would escalate to family services. I knew Jamie and his mom were staying with an aunt, but I'd told the cops they needed to check in with them. They took my opinion seriously as an educator, and I hoped that was enough.

I'd never heard such hatred in a parent's voice. How was his hate for the world so much bigger than his son's well-being?

Even at home, I felt unsettled, and sleep was elusive, so I reached for my phone to send a message for Walker to wake up to. A joke, something not serious, something I could laugh about. Instead of typing, I hit the call button. It rang only once before he answered, his voice warm and instantly reassuring.

"Finn, hey."

I sighed softly, feeling my tension ease slightly at the sound of his voice. "Hey. Were you asleep?"

"Nah, watching game film on the Champlain Fusiliers for tomorrow."

"Shit, I didn't mean to interrupt."

"You're never an interruption," he said firmly. Then, more gently, he added, "You sound tense. What's wrong?"

I hesitated, unsure how much to share, but Walker's quiet patience encouraged me. "There's this kid at school, and there's some... I can't... I don't know where to start... but there was a confrontation with his father and... I just needed to hear your voice."

Walker's voice immediately sharpened, protective. "A parent causing trouble? Did he hurt you? Threaten you?"

"No, nothing like that exactly, just... " I paused, swallowing the lingering anxiety. "He was just there outside school, so I called 911 and reported it, but... "

"Dammit, Finn," Walker mumbled, his voice tight. "What do you need? You want me to be outside the school daily? Just tell me, and I will be."

His protective streak warmed me deeply, calming my racing heart. "No, it's okay. It's handled. It just unnerved me that a parent could have so much hate in them for their own family."

I waited for him to comment, but he was very quiet, and the silence was weird. Had I been cut off? I glanced at my screen. Nope, we were still connected.

"You still there?" I asked.

"Yeah, sorry. Here."

"So, I wanted to hear your voice," I said to break the silence and remind him I was there.

"Always," he said. "You know you can call me anytime, right?"

"I know," I whispered, smiling despite myself. "How was your day, though? Tell me something good."

He chuckled, the sound instantly relaxing me. "Well, I spent most of my day helping Bob with glitter and thinking about this art teacher I know. I heard he's a big fan of hockey now."

I laughed, the tension finally draining from me. "I think he might just be a big fan of you."

Walker's voice grew soft, tender. "Good. Because I'm pretty sure I'm his biggest fan too."

We talked for an hour, shifting from serious to silly, and by the time we finally said goodnight, I felt calmer. I'd done everything I could, and I had to rely on the people who could do something by carrying out their jobs. Jamie was my student, my responsibility, and with the cops and school aware that his dad was a drunken, threatening asshole, there wasn't much else I could do. I curled up in bed, and all I could think about was Walker. I knew I was falling for him—hard and fast—in ways I'd never anticipated. The idea sent a gentle thrill through me, but it was also frightening. Walker had a past, his struggles, and the counselor part of me worried about moving too fast or expecting too much.

But as for the part that thought of Walker's quiet smiles, funny stories, sexy *hockeyness*—not that this was a word—and steady presence? Well, that part knew this was something real, and I closed my eyes, picturing Walker's soft expression and the tenderness in his touch.

I knew I was falling for Walker.

THIRTEEN

Walker

THE GAME AGAINST CHAMPLAIN WAS NOT ONE OF MY best.

I was glad it was an away game. Finn didn't have to sit in the stands and watch me be a total moron. The whole incident with that asshole parent threatening my man had stirred up something I'd thought I'd had under control. Obviously not, since I ended up with a five-minute major for fighting in the first, an elbowing call in the second, and two roughing calls in the third. The first roughing call was against the same shithead I had inadvertently elbowed in the second. Is it my fault I'm tall and that guy is short? Is it my fault that his head is where a normal man's elbow is? Nope. Still, the refs had been hitting me hard. I guess I had a reputation. Who knew? Well,

I knew, and while I usually snickered at the bullshit calls, last night's had gotten me a dressing down of biblical proportions.

At the advice of my head coach—advice being delivered with his sweaty red face directly in mine—I was sitting in the mellow environs of Dr. Quackers' office staring at him fixing us a pot of some sort of funky smelling tea. It was too damn early for this tea shit. I'd not even had morning skate yet. Not that Coach would have allowed me to skate until I'd checked in with Dr. Quackers.

"Now, this is a sipping tea," he informed me as he passed the tiny cup on the equally small saucer to me. It looked like a kid's toy in my massive mitts. "To receive its full benefits, you should enjoy it slowly. Savor it. Try not to throw it back as you normally do."

"It smells like Arnaud's skates." There was no way I was putting this shit into my body.

Says the man who routinely used to do poppers.

Point taken.

"Oh? Does Arnaud have lemon-scented skates?"

I was in no mood for funny banter with my therapist. "Not even close." I took a taste and let it flow down my throat. Yeah, I wasn't feeling it. "So, about my fall from the wagon… "

"Mm, yes, you mentioned there was an incident at the game in Champlain." He sat back, crossed his skinny legs, and tucked his goatee into the neck of his turtleneck. Then, he picked up his tea from the side table beside his chair and looked at me through curling steam tendrils. "What do you think precipitated that outburst?"

"There's this guy where Finn works, a kid's dad, and he keeps showing up at night to harass Finn. Guess the guy is a real dick. Abusive. You know?"

He merely nodded and sipped, really loud, slurpy sips that were already working on my nerves. "Has Finn called the police?"

"Sure, yeah, he's doing all the right protocols and shit, but I honestly… " I gazed down at the tea in my dainty cup. "Yeah, I honestly want to hang out in the school parking lot every night now."

"What would you do in the parking lot at Finn's school?"

"Guard Finn. And when Mr. Asshole Dad arrived, I could show him how it feels to be on the receiving end of an ass whipping." My gaze lifted from the putrid lemon tea to my counselor. The good doctor stared back at me, quirking a thick eyebrow. "That's it. I just want to punch the guy in the face numerous times."

"I see." He loud slurped again. A little chime clock over on his desk rang.

I waited. He sipped and slurped. I waited some more. "That's all you have to say? I see? I mean, the team is paying you all kinds of money to talk with me, and so far today, all you've done is sit there and slurp tea. Also, and this is almost as annoying as you slurping, is the fact that you tucked your silly goatee into your shirt. So, you look like a turtle in a turtleneck drinking tea that smells like my friend's rotten skates."

"I'm meeting my wife for lunch today and she dislikes it when I have tea dried in my goatee." I blinked. "I can tie a napkin around it if that would be better?"

"No, that would not be better. That would be worse." I placed the cup and saucer on the coffee table none too gently. "I feel like you're just phoning this session in, to be honest. Like, shouldn't you be telling me that the incident with Finn and that asshole has got me so fired up because it's stirring up memories of when my dad was being an abusive prick to me, and that by me hitting people it purges the built-up anger that I feel toward my father, who didn't even have the fucking courage to face me man-to-man, but died before I was big enough to beat him down?" I blurted and drew in a breath. He just sat there, slurp-sipping. "Shouldn't you be telling me that I need to process all of this with methods we've discussed instead of driving my elbow into the head of some Hobbit on skates? Why aren't you reminding me that violence is not the healthy way to work through the pain?!"

"I don't need to ask you those questions, as you've already answered them for yourself." He smiled serenely at me and took another sip. Well, fuck me sideways. "You should try the tea again. It will grow on you."

"You're a sneaky shit. Stop making me heal myself." I picked up the fucking tea and took another taste. Yeah, nope, it was terrible. It made me pucker. I hated it. "So how do I stop wanting to hurt my father as much as he hurt me?"

"We'll work on that. For now, let's sip tea and talk about some coping mechanisms for when you feel that dark urge to lash out at fantasy characters on ice skates."

This guy was a total flake. I kind of liked him, though. I'd never tell him that, obviously.

COACH WORKED ME SO HARD AT MORNING SKATE I'D like to have died. I mean, *shit, dude*. Morning skate was supposed to be light. Guess he was still pissed about my penalty minutes, which was legit. After I crawled off the ice, I managed to get undressed, showered, and pulled on my street clothes. My hamstrings were still burning when I was easing my arms into my coat. The other art guys were hanging around the dressing room as I limped around looking for my other sneaker. I threw a dark look at Arnaud when it turned up in the soda cooler.

"I think maybe it would chill out your hothead?" he offered with a playful smirk and shrug.

"My head is on the other end of my body, dipshit," I snarled, then shoved my foot into an icy cold Nike.

"Hey, be grateful it was your shoe. It could have been your jock," Bob said with a pointed look at our impish second-string tendie. "You feel down to go get some lunch? I'm buying."

"I don't know. I'm mentally and physically done."

"We can bring some stuff to your place," Chip said softly and, while I wasn't really into being personable right now, the offer of friendship was too hard to pass up. Besides, Finn was in school and Harper was working, so I'd just be sitting around my place alone, being a sullen shit. Why not have the guys over?

"Sure, yeah," I said. An hour later, we filled my living room, big burly guys spread out over the sectional sofa stuffing Chinese into their mouths. No beer allowed. Just water to wash it down. Someone had suggested tea. That was a hard no from me. I'd had enough tea during my session with the quack man.

"About the last game," I flung out when a conversation about the latest episode of a fantasy show we all watched dipped off. "I really fucked up. I know I cost us the game with that late penalty."

"Meh, shit happens. We all fuck up," Bob said. He was just being nice because he was my defensive partner.

"Oui, you did fuck it up," Arnaud agreed before slurping some lo mein noodles into his mouth. "But we all do that on occasion," he tacked on after swallowing.

"Yeah, well, I'm letting my personal shit interfere with hockey. I can't do that anymore if I ever want to get back to New York, but sometimes…" I lowered my chopsticks back into the white takeout box of sweet and sour pork. "My childhood was pretty dismal. My dad was a shit. Abusive. I have some major anger issues. I'm totally screwed up."

"I have emotional dysregulation," Bob muttered into his container of beef and broccoli. "But yeah. Anger issues."

"My best friend died, and I have these crippling anxiety attacks," Taft shared over his wonton soup.

"I'm neurodivergent," Chip whispered while tapping at the side of his box five times before picking up more noodles with his chopsticks. He did that before every bite. "I don't understand social shit, then I get anxious." He took another bite, chewed, then added, "About 80 percent of autistic adults experience clinically significant anxiety."

I reached over to touch the side of his knee gently. Just enough to let him know we were there, and we kind of got it.

"I am always making a goof to make people happy, to laugh, but that is to cover up a bad childhood where I was made fun of for my teeth. They were quite bad. Now they are new and straight, but... ah, you know, children are cruel." Arnaud sighed, then lifted more noodles to his mouth.

"Damn, we are fucked-up art guys," I said a moment later, after my brain absorbed all the secrets that had spilled out. "Thanks for sharing, guys. It, uhm… it means a lot."

"Yeah, well, no point in you feeling like the odd duck. We're all quackers," Bob tossed out, which led Arnaud into a tale about taking rotten duck eggs from an old nest as a child.

He'd planned to take them to school to toss out during an assembly, but they broke in his backpack on the school bus. The bus had to be evacuated. The kids thought it was hilarious, but the bus driver and Arnaud's parents, not so much. We all laughed heartily, so maybe we were just boys at heart still? I wasn't sure, but I *was* sure that this small band of misfits was quickly becoming something very important to me. As was Finn. How I was going to leave them when I went back to Broadway, I had no clue…

———

"Hey, stop picking up," I called to Finn that night as he puttered around my apartment gathering up empty white boxes and water bottles. "Come sit down here with me." I patted the sofa. He glanced around the messy living room, his hands filled with cartons. "Come. Sit. I need a few kisses. Let Harper clean that up when she gets home."

"That is so sexist," Finn gasped, but he placed the takeout containers back on the coffee table before sitting down on me as opposed to the couch. A move that I was very much agreeable with.

"It's also funny because Harper is a bigger slob than I could ever hope to be," I informed him as my hands came to rest on his sides. "We'll bicker over who has to clean the place this weekend, then we'll just make a fast push through and call it good."

"As long as someone cleans," he said as his fingers threaded into my hair. His sweet little ass rested on my thighs. If I moved him up just an inch or two, his groin would be tight to my belly.

"Someone will. Eventually." I nestled him closer and captured his mouth. He opened quickly, eager for the kiss, his tongue curling around mine. My grip tightened, keeping him in place as our cocks began to thicken. "God, you feel good in my arms," I panted when the kiss broke. He nipped at my lower lip and got wiggly. The rub of his dick against mine made me hiss in pleasure.

He wriggled around like a worm, sucking on my neck as he pulled at my shirt. I was fully into this bossy side of him, so I lifted my arms. Up and off my shirt went. The shy art teacher now looked down at my chest with a hunger that made him bold.

"You have a lot of hair," he whispered as his thumbs flicked over my nipples, sending a jolt of 220-current to my balls. "I love that. Can I rub my face on you?"

"You can do whatever you want to me." That got me a lusty smile. He began a slow slither to the floor, pausing to bury his nose into the dark curls on my chest. He sucked my nipples loudly, nibbled a path down to my joggers, and then lifted molten hazel eyes to me. "May I suck your cock?"

"Yeah, please." What else did you say when the world's sexiest man asked to gobble your prick? I might not be the brightest bulb in the chandelier, but I wasn't stupid either. He freed my dick with a gentle tug of the strings holding my pants on my hips. He wet his lips when he saw it, the head slick with precum and dark purple. "Like what you see?"

"Gorgeous." I may have blushed. Yeah, I had a nice dick. Not the biggest in the world but girthy enough to give anyone who sat on it a wild ride. He placed his tongue on the underside and licked down to the root before laving a sloppy path back to my slit. After that, he stretched his lips over the head.

Goddamn, he looked good with my dick in his mouth. Stuff of dreams.

"Oh shit," I moaned, head falling back to the sofa when he took me down his throat. The man knew how to fellate. I grabbed the throw pillows from the sofa. Two ugly yellow things that Harper had picked up at a thrift shop over by the Seneca Park Zoo last week and squeezed them instead of his head. I wasn't a fan of people grabbing my head when I went down on them, so I liked to repay the favor. His tongue swirled around my cockhead, over and over, as his hands massaged my thighs. My balls were tight in no time. I really did not want to blow a nut so quickly, but it had been months since I'd gotten off with someone other than Patty Palm. "Finn... I'm so close... "

He hummed around my dick, and that was all it took. My balls tightened, and my ass left the sofa cushion. His fingers bit into my thighs as he took every drop that pulsed out of me. My back arched while my feet tried to find purchase on the carpet. Winded as if I had done a bag skate with a hippo on my shoulders, I lay there spread out like a soggy noodle as he gave a few licks to clean the spunk from my dick. Somehow, I managed to get my head up enough to look down at him: brown-green eyes glowing, chin shiny with spittle, and his lips dark red.

He wiped those glossy lips with the back of his hand. "You are so beautiful," he said, his voice hoarse from having my cock down his throat. At that, something clicked inside my head. A lock that opened up a creaky door to a dismal, dank closet packed full of terrible crap.

"Men aren't beautiful. Why do you say such stupid shit?" It fell out of me with such speed it took us both aback. Finn, resting on his heels, stared at me in shock. Shit. *Fuck*. "Don't say that kind of shit." I tucked my cock away and got up, moving awkwardly to clear his head with my leg, then I fumbled to my feet, my legs weak from that workout this morning.

"Walker… " I shook my head. Fucking hell. Why did this shit pop out of my damn mouth at the worst fucking times? What the fuck was wrong with me?! I thunked my brow with the heel of my hand.

"I need some air." I ripped my coat off the rack and was out the door before he was even properly on his feet. The elevator was too slow. I bolted to the stairs and, then, out a side door, the wind off Lake Ontario greeting me like the wild banshee that she could be in the winter. It nearly knocked me back into the complex, but I forged on, shoulder into the wind, nose running, eyes watering, wretched things bubbling inside my head. Bad things. Things that I did not want to subject a kind, loving man like Finn to.

I walked and walked. Bitter cold gusts pushed against me until I reached the Rochester Harbor, where the Genesee River flowed into the great lake. Commercial boats with rows of lights could be seen reflected on the lake's choppy surface. I turned my face into the wind to look at the marina, where hundreds of recreational boats could be found in warmer weather. Most were off the lake now since the water did freeze. There was no ice yet, so the big boats were all business as usual.

Hands in my pockets, I shivered as the light from the Charlotte-Genesee lighthouse helped to guide ships into the harbor. My phone lay on the end table, so it was just me and the spirits of the rumored ghost ships that sailed the great lake.

Finn would be worried. Maybe I should tell him. Just spill all the shitty deets about my past. Tell him I was beaten as a child and let him decide if he was able to date a man with such a fucked-up head. Or, and this was probably the best thing for all, I should just let him find someone who wasn't a grade A basket case. It would be for the best. For him, not for me obviously, but for him. He was too good to be loving a man who was such a piece of shit.

I stood there for so long my feet and fingers had grown numb, and the first subtle shades of dawn were pinkening the sky. Limping home, I crept into my place, seeing Harper's coat on the rack, and Finn gone. My cell lay dead on the end table. I plugged it in to charge, numb inside and out, and read over the dozen texts from Finn. Each one filled with concern, apologies, and so much caring that I wanted to weep, but men didn't cry. I fired off one reply to him.

Walker: I'm a fuckup. Can we meet tomorrow after school 2 talk? If U don't want to I understand. ~ W

I dragged myself into the shower. There I stood under the hot flow until the stream began to cool, and then I made my way to bed. I lay there and watched the sun fully rise, my toes still cold, and came to the conclusion that I needed to tell Finn the truth about my past. He had earned that at the very least. Truthfully, he had earned way more, but it was all I had to give him.

FOURTEEN

Finn

It had been a long day, one of those never-ending Friday afternoons where the minutes dragged, and the air in the classroom felt stale and heavy. What had happened with Walker had thrown me for a loop. I'd tried to get ahold of him, but his message about meeting after school made me worry and fret and get excited all at the same time. Maybe that was why the kids were restless. Or maybe they were eager for the weekend, and honestly, so was I. Jamie sat quietly at his table, drawing, head bent low over the paper. His fingers clutched the crayon tight. I'd spent all week watching him closely, catching how he'd flinch if someone walked too close or how he stared off into space for far too long.

He was having counseling, his mom too, his dad not part of their lives.

I'd been kept in the loop, but I hated it all. Poor kid.

When the last bell rang, I let out a sigh of relief. Most of the kids burst from the room, laughing and shouting while they bolted for their parents as they collected them. Being this is grade one, the parents came to the side door, but it was evident that no one came for Jamie.

"Hey, buddy," I said softly. "Your mom should be here soon."

He didn't look up. He just added a streak of black over what I realized was a drawing of his house. The windows were dark this time, and the sky above it was all scribbles. A cold knot twisted in my stomach.

"She's late," Jamie mumbled.

"I'm sure she's caught in traffic," I said, more to reassure myself than him. "Why don't you come help me tidy up while we wait?"

Jamie nodded reluctantly, setting his drawing aside. As he helped gather stray pencils and stack chairs, I stepped into the hallway to call his mom. Straight to voicemail. Twice. After the second time, I left a message, reminding her that school let out twenty minutes ago.

I glanced at the clock for what felt like the hundredth time. Twenty minutes past dismissal, and there was still no sign of Jamie's mom. Not even a call or message, and the growing silence in the hallway only heightened my anxiety.

"Do you think she forgot me?" he whispered, his voice thin and brittle.

I knelt to Jamie's level, touching his back gently. "No way, buddy. Your mom wouldn't forget you. You're way too important."

Jamie finally lifted his head, wide-eyed and worried. "Then, why isn't she here?"

I swallowed the sudden lump in my throat, forcing a reassuring smile. "Maybe she's just running late?"

He nodded slowly, setting his crayon down. I handed him a small pile of books. "Can you put these back on the shelf for me?"

Jamie took them quietly, moving toward the shelves by the window. I stepped just outside the classroom door into the empty hall, taking a deep breath as I redialed Jamie's mother. It clicked to voicemail once more. I left another calm but firm message.

"Hi, it's Mr. Carter again. Jamie's here with me, and we were expecting you at dismissal. Please call back or come by as soon as you get this message. Jamie's doing just fine. We're just waiting for you."

None of this felt right. The last time she hadn't made it to the school, his aunt came instead. Okay, this is stupid, I muttered to myself as anxiety over why she was late coiled in my stomach. Turning back into the classroom, I plastered on a reassuring smile, hoping I could fake it with Jamie.

I pulled a chair down from the stack and decided to distract him with a simple coloring project, something safe and quiet that might keep his mind from spiraling. The scratch of the crayons on paper had just begun when a sudden crash echoed down the empty hallway. It was sharp, violent, like glass shattering.

Jamie's head snapped up, eyes wide and terrified. "What was that?" he whispered, his voice trembling as he stood up.

My gut clenched. He was always so damn scared, so quick to assume the worst, and I wanted to shield him from everything. I pulled him into a hug, pressing my cheek to his hair. "Probably just the janitor," I said, trying for casual reassurance even though my pulse was hammering hard in my throat.

Still, I couldn't shake the sound. It hadn't been a

mop bucket or a door closing. It had been brittle, final, dangerous.

I edged toward the classroom door and cracked it open, peering out into the dim corridor. The silence on the other side was too heavy, too complete. Unease prickled at my skin. Quickly, I shut the door and turned back to Jamie—

Only for it to slam open with such force, the gust shoved me off balance, stumbling me sideways. It ferociously banged against the wall.

Jamie yelped and scrambled back, then froze like a deer in headlights, his wide eyes locked on the doorway.

"Dad?"

I immediately got my footing and positioned myself protectively between him and the door where his dad leaned, bloodshot eyes and a gun in his hand.

I pressed the emergency button on my phone.

Staring down Jamie's dad, my voice was steady but urgent, and I took a chance and shouted, "Gladwell Elementary. Shooter present." Honestly, I don't know if it went to 911 since I couldn't see the screen or hear if an operator picked up.

"Drop the fucking phone!" Jamie's father yelled, waving his gun. I did as he demanded, placing it on a table, face down, hopefully still connected to the operator.

He stepped further into the classroom, his movements erratic, his breathing heavy. "Jamie, we're leaving now."

"Jamie, go to the emergency cupboard," I said, keeping my voice quiet but firm, my hand resting on his shoulder to guide him backward. His eyes were wide, darting toward the door, but I held his gaze. "Remember the lockdown drills we practiced?"

He swallowed hard, nodding just a little.

"Come here, Jamie!" his dad yelled. So fucking loud.

"You go inside, shut the door, and lock it. Then, you hide behind the big metal shelf where nobody can see you. No talking, no moving, like we practiced," I calmly explained to Jamie, knowing how scared he was.

"I don't wanna!" Jamie cried.

"Jamie! You get your ass over here now." His dad tried to get past me, and I blocked him as best I could.

"You're the best hider, Jamie, remember? Go."

Always standing between him and his dad, I nudged him back toward the cupboard we always used for drills, the one the teachers had called the *safe place*.

My heart hammered in my chest, memories of countless active shooter drills racing through my mind. The drills were weekly, the fear constant, but I had never expected it to happen—not here, not now. This was a class of babies, and they were my kids, my responsibility.

"Don't you move, son!" Jamie's dad yelled, but Jamie yelped and scampered toward the cupboard, and I waited for the lock to click.

"You're not taking my son," Jamie's dad slurred, the gun shaking in his unsteady hand. "You think you can play hero? He's coming home with me."

I stepped back slowly, keeping Jamie's Dad's focus on me instead of his son, buying time until someone, *anyone*, could help. "Let's just stay calm. You don't have to do this. Jamie needs you safe, not like this."

"Shut up!" he yelled, the gun raised slightly. "Don't tell me what my son needs!"

I backed up another step, sideways, away from the cupboard. If bullets flew, I didn't want them to pierce through the walls even as reinforced as they were. Every instinct screamed to protect Jamie at all costs.

My mind raced. If the call had connected, then what would the response time be? Would any cops even come in here to help me when Jamie's dad was armed? I'm supposed to be brave. I'm supposed to be the calm one, the one in control, but my hands trembled, and my heart pounded against my ribs. I'd done all I could to protect Jamie and guide him to safety as we'd practiced, but standing face-to-face with the unpredictable danger of an armed man, the fear was raw and overwhelming. I was terrified, but I couldn't let it show now. I had to hold on just a little longer.

"Get out of my way," Jamie's dad snarled, closing the distance between us. His breath was sour. His pupils were pinpricks.

"You're not taking him anywhere," I said.

"I'll shoot you to get to him," his dad hissed.

"Cops are on their way," I lied, my voice shaking, but I refused to back down.

Something caught my eye over the man's shoulder at the classroom door. Was it the cops? Fuck. No. Wait!

Walker!

What was Walker doing here?!

He appeared in the doorway, barely visible as he peered around the corner, his hand rising quickly, sharply signaling "shhh" with his fingers. My breath caught, and fear spiked so fiercely that I nearly shouted. My mind raced. If Jamie's dad saw him, things could turn deadly. My heart continued to hammer in my chest, panic clawing at the edges of my thoughts. Get out, Walker. Go get help, please, I silently begged him. Walker wasn't trained in how to deal with a shooter in a school. I had to de-escalate.

"How about we talk, Mr. Evans. We don't want to scare Jamie—"

"Fuck you!" Jamie's dad yelled.

Walker was out of sight. Thank fuck. Relief threatened to buckle my knees.

Then, as casually as anything, Walker strode back into the classroom as if he owned the place. "Hi, Finn," he announced brightly, voice firm but almost lazy. Jamie's dad whirled to face the new arrival.

As he stepped forward, Walker's eyes widened in mock surprise, hands raised high in fake surrender. "Whoa, whoa, what's going on here?" he said, voice shaky and uncertain, bending a little to make himself seem smaller.

"Who the fuck are you?" Jamie's dad barked, swinging the gun toward Walker.

"Me? No one," Walker stammered, stepping closer carefully. He shifted slightly, angling his body until I realized what he was doing—putting himself directly between me and the gun.

"Fuck no," I grumbled under my breath, panic

rising. I was now completely hidden behind Walker's broad, muscled back.

"What's wrong?" Walker asked, voice still light, playing dumb. "Are you okay, man? You look like you've had a rough day."

"I said, who the hell are you?" Jamie's dad spat.

"I'm nobody," Walker insisted, voice still high with fake fear.

"I want my kid! Jamie! Come out here now, you little shit!"

Walker stepped closer. "Hey, man. We can talk this out."

"Get away from the fucking teacher!" Jamie's dad growled and lunged forward to press the gun against Walker's head. Walker moved like lightning, grabbing his wrist and twisting it sharply. Jamie's dad gasped in pain, the fight draining from him as Walker wrenched his arm behind his back and pinned him against the wall, causing him to drop his gun.

I kicked the gun, which skittered across the floor and slid under the dinosaur display in the corner. My heart pounded so fiercely that I thought my chest might explode. My breath came in quick, ragged bursts, and my legs threatened to give out. Panic surged, making my hands shake as I grabbed my phone. I barely remembered lifting it to my ear, my voice frantic. "Hurry, please, oh God, hurry!"

Jamie's dad fought like a cornered animal, thrashing wildly, scratching and biting like a wildcat and drawing blood from Walker. He didn't falter. With his muscles flexing, he had Jamie's dad restrained as he cursed and struggled. Once Walker had him completely immobile, I caught snatches of what Walker was cursing into his ear—low, furious words filled with barely controlled rage.

"You're a fucking father," Walker ground out between clenched teeth. "And you wanna bruise your son? Hurt him? Fucking kill him? I should tear you apart limb from fucking limb. Preying on kids, scaring the shit out of a child… "

His grip tightened, and Jamie's dad yelped in pain, face pressed hard against the wall. "But I won't," Walker muttered darkly. "Because Jamie's got to believe there's something better than men like you."

The wail of sirens pierced the air. Within seconds, officers swarmed the room, shouting commands. "Hands up! Both of you!" one of them barked. As the officers advanced, Walker froze, lifting his hands, and they treated him as part of the threat.

"Wait!" I cried, grabbing Walker's arm. "He's

with me. He helped me!" My voice cracked with urgency, and one of the officers hesitated, glancing between us. "He stopped him. He saved us," I insisted. Slowly, they lowered their weapons, one of the officers stepping forward to cuff Jamie's dad instead and dragging him away. Only when he was gone did I go to Jamie.

"Jamie, it's okay. You can come out now," I said against the door. Walker was hovering behind me, still in protector mode.

"I want my mommy!" Jamie wailed from inside.

"She'll be here soon, Jamie. You need to come out now."

I knelt as the cupboard door creaked open. Jamie's face was blotchy, his eyes wide and glassy with shock. His legs buckled as he stumbled forward, then his breath hitched. His hands twisted into the fabric of his shirt, knuckles white, as if holding himself together was the only thing keeping him from shattering. He stumbled out, shaking so hard his teeth chattered. His whole body trembled as he staggered forward, blinking rapidly.

"Where's my mommy?" Jamie's voice was barely above a whisper, raw and broken. "I want my mommy."

"It's all good," I lied, my voice breaking. I had no

way of knowing if his mom was even alive, and I hoped to hell she was found okay. I reached out, but he flinched, his little hands curling into fists. Tears streaked his face, and he sucked in quick, panicked breaths, his chest heaving.

"I want my mommy," he repeated, sobbing now.

Jamie's aunt appeared in the doorway, her face pale. When he saw her, he ran to her, and she caught him in her arms. Her eyes met mine, wide with shock and gratitude.

"Where's my mommy!" Jamie sobbed.

"She's okay," his aunt reassured. As she mouthed, "Hospital. Okay," relief flooded me so hard my legs nearly gave out. Jamie burrowed closer to her, his tiny hands gripping her sweater like a lifeline. Seeing him safe in her arms was the moment my fear finally broke.

Walker hovered nearby, keeping watch until the police took my statement. He held my hand, and I waited as he gave his statement. We agreed to go to the station tomorrow for a formal interview since Principal Lewis was waiting for us in the hall.

"How did he get in?" I demanded of her as soon as she'd finished talking to a cop, my voice shaking with disbelief and fury. "We have lockdown procedures, we had security, we had… " I trailed off, choking on the words. "How did he get in?"

Principal Lewis swallowed hard, her voice brittle. "He forced the side door open. Broke the glass and let himself in. The silent alarm triggered, but he was in before anyone could do anything." Her eyes were bright with tears, and she rubbed a shaking hand down her face. "The cops are speaking to the security company now."

I glanced toward the hallway where officers lingered, their radios crackling as they controlled the growing crowd of reporters outside. Bright camera lights flashed against the windows, and through it all, the overwhelming sense of disbelief clung to me like a second skin. This wasn't supposed to happen. Not here. Not at my school.

Not with my kids.

Walker put his arm over my shoulder, pulling me close, his warmth grounding me in a way I hadn't realized I needed. I let myself breathe for the first time in what felt like forever, but it had only been ten minutes or less. I clenched my eyes shut, trying to hold back the tears. I didn't notice how tightly I'd been wound until now, not until I felt his solid presence beside me, reminding me I wasn't alone. The fear, the helplessness, all of it began to crack open inside me. My fingers twisted into his shirt, and he held me tight as though afraid to let go.

"How did you know to come?" My voice wavered, still raw with everything that had happened.

"I was here to say sorry," he admitted. "But when the secretary ran out, screaming that there was a shooter… " He trailed off, shaking his head. "I couldn't leave you and the kid in here." His voice was low, rough around the edges, as if he'd barely kept himself together. I stared at him, my heart hammering in my chest. The words landed hard, sticking in my throat. He couldn't leave me. Walker could've been killed, and yet he'd walked in here without hesitation. Because of me. Because of Jamie. Because he couldn't turn away. I didn't know whether to hug him or scream at him.

"You should have left," I said. "Waited for the cops… you didn't have to put yourself in danger."

"I couldn't." Walker's voice was firm now, low and steady. "I couldn't walk away. I couldn't let another kid suffer like… like I did." His voice broke, the words catching in his throat.

I closed my eyes briefly, swallowing hard before leaning closer and pressing my forehead to his shoulder. My breath hitched, and suddenly, everything I'd held back—the fear, the panic, the helplessness—

surged up inside me. My fingers twisted into his shirt, gripping tight as though he was the only thing keeping me upright.

"And I couldn't… I couldn't let anyone hurt the man I love," Walker confessed, his voice rough with emotion. His words hit me like a lightning bolt, cracking open something I hadn't even realized I'd kept locked away.

"What?" My voice barely worked, a whisper that caught in my throat. "You love me?"

Walker huffed a small, breathless laugh, then pressed a lingering kiss to my head. "From the moment you faced a classroom of puck pushers and faced all that anger, I loved your fire, your courage… and I… I just… it was easy… I love you."

I blinked rapidly, too overwhelmed to say anything meaningful. Instead, I squeezed him tighter, whispering, "I love you, too."

He exhaled, the tension in his body finally unraveling. "Let's go back to your place, yeah?"

FIFTEEN

Walker
_____

FINN WAS BADLY SHAKEN.

After the cops were done with us, I curled over my guy like a protective eagle curling its wings around their chick and shouldered our way through the press corps shouting questions at us. I led Finn to my car, got him in, closed the door, and spun to face the thicket of reporters. Bright lights from the rolling cameras made me wince as I addressed the reporters desperate for a story.

"Mr. Carter and I are not commenting at this time at the advice of the Rochester police." That was a lie. The cops had not told us anything, but I had to assume that the criminal justice system would work better if we didn't go blabbering to the press about what happened. If we deviated one inch from our statements, it could fuck things up when things went to trial. And I *so* wanted this piece of shit to go to trial. I could taste the need for retribution on my tongue. It was metallic and cold like old blood. "We ask that you respect his need for privacy at this most upsetting time."

And with that, I nudged a guy asking me about my relationship with the teacher aside as only a hockey player can nudge. If not for a random cameraman behind him, that reporter would have been planted in the snowbank. When I got into my car, I locked the doors, cranked her over, and off we went, sending the press scattering to get out of the way.

"Fucking vultures," I grumbled as my seat belt alarm pinged steadily. "It was the same in New York after that whole twink incident that got me sent down." I threw Finn a look as we slowed at a stop sign to leave the school grounds. I shoved the belt into the latch plate and the pinging stopped. "You okay?"

He looked pasty. "Just cold." His hazel eyes locked with mine. "What twink incident?"

Well shit. I had a lot to tell him. But not right now. "I'll tell you everything when we get to your place, okay?" He nodded. His slim shoulders drawn to his ears. "We'll have heat soon."

"You handled them well," he whispered as we sped toward his little apartment complex.

"I have experience with the press."

"Right, playing in New York would give you practical knowledge," he replied as he shivered. The heater was still blowing chilly air, so I pulled up at the next light and peeled off my coat. "No, you should keep that."

"I spend 80 percent of my life on ice. I have the constitution of a polar bear. You need it more." I draped it around him despite his weak protests. With a hum of pleasure, he pulled it on, burrowing into the oversized coat like a chilly little eaglet. I really needed to stop watching eagle nest hatchling videos in my downtime. "There. Better?"

"Much." He pulled the collar of the cocoa-colored shearling coat up to his nose. Given that it was an XXL plus extra tall, he was lost in it. If we weren't still mentally fried from what had happened a few hours ago, I would have felt all kinds of randy seeing my tiny guy in my big coat. Right now, though, my libido had checked out. Maybe it would reappear later. I hoped.

We rode along in silence, the radio playing some

old '60s hits. Finn was lost in his head, gazing at the wintry streets. The shivering had stopped anyway. When we pulled into his drive, he sat there staring at his place as if he wasn't sure where he was.

"He was going to shoot us." Finn's voice cracked as he spoke. I left my truck running while we sat there, hot air blowing so hard on our faces my eyes were dried out and my nose felt like sandpaper.

"Let's get you inside, baby."

He nodded, a few tears sliding down his cheek. The truck ticked as the engine cooled while I got him out of the truck and through his front door. He found the lights. Then, he looked up at me at his side, my arm around his middle.

"I can walk." He padded away, leaving me at the front door. I toed off my sneakers and followed him to the tasteful living room. He flopped down on the sofa, the furred collar of my coat resting on his ashen cheeks. "I could use a drink."

"Yeah, I feel that. I would love a stiff one myself, but booze and my mellow pills don't mix. Can I make some coffee?"

"Right, yes, of course. You can't drink. Please, coffee. Cream is in the fridge."

"Got it. You just rest, baby."

"Can you check the doors and windows? To make sure they're all locked?"

"Totally can do that." I knew that fear well. Many were the nights Harper and I had lain in bed, me cuddling her to me, my face bruised from a beating, startling at every little noise. Trauma made a soul jumpy.

His kitchen was cute. The appliances were older but well taken care of. The fridge was covered with pictures of him and his students as well as some of him and his brother. Drawings from his students, awards from the school. He was so beloved. Not just by me either.

I took a moment to text Harper to let her know that I was okay and that there might be some news flowing into her feed with my name in it. I promised I would talk to her in the morning. She was out on a date with some guy she worked with. She'd been flirting hard with the guy for weeks, and so, she was probably busy getting her freak on with said dude. A dude I hadn't met yet, but then, she hadn't met Finn either, so that was tit for tat or whatever they said.

I turned off my phone.

As the coffee perked, I did a sweep of his home. Nice place, a little on the small side and somewhat old, but it was Finn all over. When I returned to the kitchen, I poured two mugs, creamed them, and toted them to the living room. Finn was right where I had left him, still wearing my coat, and all that I could see were his little nose and eyes.

"Did you check the windows?" he asked, carefully taking the hot mug from me.

"Yep, and the doors. No one is coming in here." I sat down beside him, thighs touching, and took a sip of my coffee. Strong as hell. Which might be a good thing because we had a long night of talking and processing to do.

"I feel as if I don't know which way to turn my thoughts. My mind touches on something, then leaps off in another direction. I can't settle my emotions or my thinking." He cradled his mug in two hands. Thankfully, they weren't trembling as badly anymore. He glanced at me from under thick lashes. "I've never felt such anger before directed at me or a child. It's… terrifying. Poor Jamie."

"Yeah," I huffed while I stared at the little statuette I'd given him sitting on the entertainment center that held his TV, a few books with cloth marks hanging out of them, and a stack of papers. "He's going to be scarred from that, but… " I turned on the sofa, knee up, arm coming to rest on the back behind his shoulders. "He had someone to stand up for him, and that will make a huge difference."

Finn shook his head. "I was too scared to do anything. You were the hero."

"Pfft. No, I was just doing what I've been doing for years. See some asshole dude trying to hurt someone you love, and you get your dumb ass in front of your loved one."

He swallowed loudly. "I know we've been through a lot tonight, and it may not be the best time for you to get into it all, so please tell me if you're too upset to talk about your childhood before I broach the subject."

"Nah, it's fine. There's no good time, baby." I gave him a flimsy smile. I suspected he was using my past to avoid having to think about what he'd just lived through. Avoidance. Something that I knew well. "It started well before either my sister or I were born. Dad was a violent man even as a child, according to a great-aunt whom we met once. Mom left after Harper was born, not a clue where she went. One time, a neighbor told us they'd seen her when they'd been in Texas visiting family, but I didn't care. She left us with him. Yeah, she was running for her life because he'd beat her for years, but… "

"I'm sorry for asking."

"No, no, I want to get this all out because I love you, and you need to know the full story before we get any more involved. This way you can tell me to take a walk out into Lake Ontario and not come back. I would not hold that against you because I am fucked up in big ways."

"I would never tell you to do that." He wiggled around to face me, tucked his feet under his backside, and reached out to take my hand. "I love you no matter what."

We'd see. Taking a deep breath, I plunged back into my timeline, something that I never did with anyone other than Dr. Quackers. I started at the beginning, when Dad had to shift his aggression to his kids because his battered wife had gone shopping for groceries and had simply disappeared off the face of the earth.

"I was six. Harper was two. The fists started flying on my seventh birthday and never stopped. Hockey was my savior in a lot of ways. It was the only thing that gave me pride. It was also a way to vent. Fighting in juniors was a no-go, but once you got older and into the pros, fighting was not only accepted, it was also cheered. Gladiatorial sport and all that. I had refused to billet in my junior days, which crimped my chances to play with better teams, but I could not leave Harper unprotected." This all came out as Finn held my hand tightly. "The whippings, the hatred of his own children for resembling his runaway wife… they became more and more frequent until I hit fifteen.

"By then, I was bigger than him, stronger. I could —and did—fight back. And I began to win the battles at home more and more until he stopped waving his fists in my face. I went to college, taking Harper with me and setting her up with a friend who lived near campus. She went to work at a diner after lying on her application, saying she was eighteen when she was really only fourteen. She began training with me at the school gym. Dad never once asked where she went or why, the bastard."

Finn nodded silently, his grip tight.

"Hockey was my game, kickboxing was hers. No one was ever going to slap us around again. Only, she could handle the Vesuvius of aggression that we carried inside of us in a productive way. Me? Meh, not so much, but every fight I had in the pros got me good press and stick taps. I was a star, fists of fury, rich and looking for an outlet for the bubbling dark goo that Dad had planted in my chest.

"When he died of a massive coronary in my senior year of college, Harper and I cheered. We never went to the funeral. Neither of us cared where he was buried. Somewhere in Maryland, according to the funeral home mailing address. I'd probably piss on his headstone if I ever stumbled across it. There was a pittance of life insurance left after the funeral director got his cut. We bought her a car for work and some new gloves for her bouts. Then it was gone. Just like him, and Mom, and all the other adults who were supposed to care but never really did."

I took a break then, looking down at the little statue with the happy teacher. "This coffee sucks balls," I confessed but downed the last cold dregs to wet my throat. "So, all of that kind of leads to the twink who tried to steal my phone last October. I lost my shit. Beat the hell out of the guy and ended up being arrested. The Vipers were not impressed. I had a rap sheet with the league already, so that was the famous straw breaking the camel's back. I got sent down here to get my shit together with the Copperheads and met you." I looked right into his dewy eyes. "The very best thing that has ever happened to me was going to that art class and meeting you. The first time I saw you... something nice and sweet took root. And you watered that seedling of possibility and fed it, gave it your sunny smile, and it grew. Why am I talking flowers?"

He smiled, a shaky one, but a smile just the same. "Because you are a beautiful man." I rolled my eyes. "You are."

"Beautiful. Not so sure that can be applied to me. But I will say that men *can* be beautiful because fuck you, Dad, and your stupid, hurtful gender norms bullshit."

"Yeah!" Finn croaked as he let his head drop to my shoulder.

"I'm sorry I flipped out when you called me beautiful. Sometimes, when I least expect it, his hate flares up like a vile weed that tries to strangle the pretty flower you planted."

"*You* planted it, Walker." He lifted his brow from my shoulder to look into my soul. "I might have moved the bushel basket to allow the sun to shine on it, but you did all the hard work to make it grow."

I kissed his nose. "I love you. I know I'm a junkyard dog, so if you get tired of my slobbering all over you or lifting my leg on the sofa or chewing up your shoes, just send me to the pound. I didn't have a really good role model for how a healthy love is supposed to be, but I promise I'll do my best. I'll bring you the paper every day and not bark at the mailman too loudly."

He chuckled before patting my face. "I love you. You're a big man with the heart of a hero. I will always keep you close and shelter you from whatever demons still haunt you. As for the mailman, I think he carries dog treats."

"Mm, I hope they're peanut butter." I pulled him under my arm. He curled into me, fitting perfectly, just like that final Lego snaps into your completed pirate ship.

"Thank you for sharing," he whispered before his empty cup slipped from his fingers. I held him there for the longest time before slipping my arms around him to lift him and carry him to his bed. He never moved as I laid him down and pulled his covers over him. It was only when I flipped the light off that he stirred. "Walker, lie with me. I'm always safest in your arms."

How could a man deny a request like that? I removed my jeans, leaving me in a tee and boxers, and climbed into bed. He freed himself from my coat, his pants and shirt, and joined me under the comforter, his cheek coming to rest on my chest.

"Close your eyes. No one will ever hurt you when I'm around. Woof," I whispered to him, but he was already asleep. I pressed a kiss on his hair, then lay there long enough to see the sun rise before my body finally shut things down. Whatever awaited us when the sun rose was going to have to just wait for a few hours…

SIXTEEN

Finn

———

I FIRST NOTICED WARMTH, SOLID AND COMFORTING
against my back, the steady rise and fall of Walker's
chest syncing with my breathing. His arm lay heavy
across my waist, his fingers curled loosely where
they'd found my hip. I didn't want to move. The
room was still, bathed in soft morning light that
filtered through the gaps in my curtains. Outside, faint
sounds of life drifted in—a car door slamming, distant
footsteps crunching on frozen snow—but here, in this
bed, it was quiet and safe.

Images from yesterday invaded my thoughts:
Jamie's pale face, the echo of shouts down the
hallway, and the cold grip of fear in my gut. I screwed
my eyes tight, trying to push it all back. Maybe I
moved, trying to shake it off, but Walker shifted

slightly behind me, his breath warming the back of my neck. He murmured something low, a soft hum that vibrated against my skin. The noise faded away, and I sank deeper into the pillow.

I could stay like this forever.

I shouldn't have been surprised when his hand flexed against my hip, sliding lower an inch at a time, his knuckles brushing bare skin. My breath caught. Walker moaned again, still half-asleep, and his hand pressed closer, fingertips dragging lightly over my belly.

"You awake?" he mumbled, voice scratchy with sleep.

"Yeah," I whispered back, barely louder than a breath.

"You okay?"

"Trying to be."

"Good." His lips found my shoulder, warm and dry, pressing lazy kisses along the curve of my neck. I arched back instinctively, nestling tighter against him. His body—solid, warm, perfect—moved with mine, fitting against me like a puzzle piece.

"I like waking up like this," I admitted quietly.

Walker chuckled, low and rough. "Me too."

He shifted again, rolling his hips forward until I felt him, thick and hard against the curve of my ass.

Heat bloomed low in my belly, and suddenly, I couldn't think of anything except how good it felt to have him this close.

"Yeah?" I teased, nudging back against him.

His breath hitched. "Yeah."

His hand slid lower, finding the waistband of my boxers, and slipped inside. He cupped me gently, just holding, his thumb brushing back and forth in slow, teasing strokes that made my pulse trip. I moaned softly, rocking my hips into his palm.

"God, you're warm," he whispered, voice rough.

"So are you." I reached back to run my hand over his hip, pulling him closer.

We found a rhythm, slow, deliberate, his hand working me, my body rocking back against his. Skin slid against skin, his cock dragging hot and heavy between my cheeks. Walker groaned, low and deep, his hips stuttering against mine.

"Finn… " His hand tightened on me just enough to make my breath shudder.

"Yeah," I gasped, my body humming with tension.

He pressed closer still, the soft grind of his cock against me driving both of us higher. His fingers moved so damn slowly and carefully, but I knew I wasn't going to last.

"Close," I choked out.

"Me too," Walker whispered in my ear, voice tight.

I pushed back hard, feeling him tense behind me as his breath caught, his body shuddering. Heat spilled between us just as I broke too, gasping his name as my release coated his hand. We stayed tangled like that for a long time, still breathing hard, my back slick with sweat where his chest pressed tightly against me.

Walker kissed the nape of my neck again, softer this time, gentle and lingering. "You okay?" he asked quietly.

I twisted to face him, sliding one arm around his waist and tugging him closer. His eyes, still heavy with sleep, softened when they met mine.

"I'm *really* okay." I sighed.

"Good." His fingers traced a lazy circle on my lower back.

"I'm glad you're here," I said softly, and I meant it more than I could explain. The words left my mouth before I knew I would tell them, raw and honest in a way that made my chest ache. I hadn't realized just how much I needed him until that moment.

Walker's lips quirked into a small, sleepy smile, softer than anything I'd ever seen from him. He leaned in, pressing a slow kiss to my mouth, and whispered against my lips, "Me too."

We lay like that for a while longer, tangled in warmth and quiet comfort, until his alarm for him to get to morning skate chased us from bed.

"It's not a heavy skate because of the Buccaneers game tonight," he said after we took turns showering, then spent a long time exchanging lazy, minty kisses in the kitchen. "I'll be back in a couple of hours... " He paused and cleared his throat. "Unless you want to come with me."

"I'm coming to the game tonight," I hurried to reassure him.

"Yeah, but you could always come watch me try not to fall over while doing sexy things on the ice."

Walker's phone buzzed. He glanced at the screen, grimaced, and muttered, "I have to take this."

He stepped away from me, his phone pressed to his ear, and I hopped off the counter and started clearing breakfast, which was nothing more than coffee and day-old pastries. The conversation was one-sided, but Walker's half carried enough information for me to piece things together.

"Yes, I tackled the guy," Walker was saying. "No, I'm not a hero... yes... I'm with Finn." He glanced at me then, catching my eyes. "We love each other... "

Harper squealed so loud I could hear her without even being close. Walker moved the phone from his ear, his eyes wide. "Jeez, Harp, you've deafened me." He chuckled then. "Yes, I'm sure. A brother... Connor... yes... I love you too, Harper... Saturday... no, we're playing a matinee game... okay... well, you book it, and we'll come... okay... bye, love you." He grinned at me. "That was Harper."

"So, I heard."

"She's booking a table at Chico's next Saturday so you can meet her properly, and she wants you to ask Connor to go too."

"Your sister's relentless," I said, amused.

"Yeah," Walker agreed, slinging his arm around my shoulders. "But she's right. I haven't met Connor yet, and I'd like to, and I want you to meet Harper. So, Saturday? Chico's?"

"Deal."

Stepping outside the house was more challenging than I expected. Last night weighed heavily on my shoulders. Even knowing Jamie's dad was likely still locked up didn't offer much comfort. Or maybe he wasn't? The thought sent a shiver down my spine. I pulled Detective Aster's card from my wallet -- which he'd handed me. As soon as I climbed into the car, I sent him a quick message.

His reply came fast:

Detective Aster: Arrested. Charged with assault, unlawful possession of a firearm, assault on school property, and endangering a minor. Refused bail. Arraignment scheduled for Monday morning.

I read it twice, the words pressing into my chest like the first real breath after holding it underwater. Charged. Refused bail. That meant he wasn't walking free anytime soon. That meant Jamie could sleep easier. So could I. But it still left a trail of unease curling in my stomach. Because the damage had already been done, and not all of it could be fixed in court.

I messaged Aster again, fingers hovering before I hit send.

Finn: Do we need to be there? Do I? Does Jamie? Do witnesses go to arraignments?

A few minutes later, he replied.

Detective Aster: Witnesses are not required to attend. They usually aren't unless the court requests, and I'll let you know if that changes. Focus on taking care of yourself right now. I'll handle the courtroom stuff. Keep your head down with the media. Your time will come to have your say.

Speaking of the media, we had to run from a group of them who'd somehow tracked down where I lived. They didn't come into the apartment block but were outside, snapping photos, shouting questions, and blocking the entrance like vultures scenting blood.

Walker didn't hesitate. He tugged a cap low over my head, pulled up the hood of my sweatshirt, and kept his body angled protectively between me and the crowd as we slipped out the side door and down the fire escape. His hand never left the small of my back.

He got me to his car fast, practically shoving me inside before slamming the door behind me. His jaw was tight, and his knuckles were white around the steering wheel as we peeled out of the lot.

"We'll get someone to fetch your clothes, then we're getting a place somewhere else," he said through gritted teeth. "Somewhere quiet."

"It's my home—" I started, but he cut me off.

"But it's not safe for a while, and, babe, you being safe is my priority." We stopped at a red light. He looked over at me, something fierce and tender burning behind his eyes. "Let me look after you?"

I opened my mouth, ready to argue, ready to say something about independence or practicality, but the look on his face silenced me. It wasn't a plea. It was a promise. I nodded slowly.

"Okay." I wasn't even going to argue.

"AND THIS IS THE LOCKER ROOM," WALKER announced, holding me back before sticking his head around the door. "Clothes on! We got company!"

There was some cursing, but when he waited for a few more seconds until he let me in, everyone was covered up. The locker room was buzzing when we walked in, the usual clang of sticks and thump of skates on concrete echoing through the space. A few guys glanced up as Walker and I entered, their conversations dropping momentarily, but there were no smirks, no whispered comments. Just nods. Respect.

The art boys crowded around one bench, taping sticks and arguing about some abstract spray paint installation one had seen over the weekend. Bob looked up first and gave us a low whistle.

"Look who's still standing after all that chaos," he said.

Walker raised an eyebrow. "I'm not the one who got tackled."

I rolled my eyes. "You did the tackling. Big difference."

Arnaud grinned. "Oui, and you are like... how you say... a freaking action hero, non?"

Walker groaned and sat in his cubby, pulling me down with him. "Not a hero. We were trying to keep a kid safe."

Chip was suddenly serious. "Statistically, intervention in high-risk situations by bystanders reduces harm by up to 43 percent. Most people freeze. You didn't." His voice was quiet, but the room stilled for a second.

Then, Arnaud nodded solemnly. "Still sounds like a hero to me."

Taft nodded. "Not everyone would've done it."

That was the end of it. No jabs, no jokes. Just respect.

When Walker and the art boys stepped onto the ice a few minutes later, the guys who were already out there noticed. Sticks tapped on the ice one by one, and the noise echoed across the practice arena—sharp, steady, and unmistakably for him.

Walker froze for a second, then glanced up, eyes wide, mouth open as though he might say something, but he didn't. He just nodded back, silent but grateful.

Coach blew his whistle. "Warm-up laps. Let's move."

Walker skated off with the others, but I caught the look on his face before he turned, something tight and shining in his expression. He didn't say it, but I knew.

They had his back.

He had my back.

Everything was okay for the moment.

Walker, ever the protector, had insisted we take a suite on the top floor of a fancy-ass hotel. "Best security," he'd said when I'd raised an eyebrow at the price tag. "And I have the money, so don't argue."

I did try to argue, but he kissed me and promised me I was his to look after and fuck, I liked that.

I liked it *a lot.* And after everything, I wasn't going to argue. It was quiet, tucked away, and I could sleep without jumping at every noise.

The arraignment was brief but loaded. Aster messaged me the moment it was done. The charges were an unlawful possession of a firearm, assault on school property, endangering a minor, and resisting arrest. Jamie's dad had pleaded not guilty, but the judge wasn't buying the act. No bail. No conditions. Remanded straight into custody.

I didn't know what justice looked like in cases like this, where damage had already been done, where trauma clung to everyone it touched, but maybe this was a start.

A FEW DAYS AFTER THE INCIDENT, I WAS BACK IN THE classroom, a temporary one, with the same set of kids, minus Jamie. He was taking some extra time but was due back on Monday. The room was different, and the vibe was more subdued. But the kids? They were resilient. They watched me carefully as if they were still waiting to see if I was okay. So, I told them I was fine, told them jokes, and held them when they got upset. I spent most of the days making their days happy.

If I went home exhausted from reliving the event in the media or having cameras outside the school, Walker was there, making things better, one hug and kiss at a time.

And now, I was meeting his sister, and he was meeting Connor, and it was surreal. The bistro Harper had booked was warm and cozy, the low hum of conversation filling the air as we followed the hostess to a corner table. Walker wasn't hiding who he was, but the place was quiet enough so that if they did know, they didn't stop talking to stare. Candles flickered on every tabletop, casting soft shadows across the walls. It smelled of garlic, wine, and something rich and buttery. Comfort food, comfort atmosphere. The kind of warm, inviting scent that wrapped around you like a blanket. After days of sterile hotel rooms, whispered conversations, and adrenaline-soaked memories, it felt like a hug I didn't know I needed. My shoulders eased a little the second we stepped in, the cozy ambience tugging me back toward something that almost felt normal. This was something we both needed after the week we'd had.

And score… there were no paparazzi.

Connor had gotten there first, seated at the table in a far corner, already nursing a beer. He stood when he saw us, giving me a quick, warm smile before turning to Walker with a more appraising look. Not unfriendly, but certainly the kind of assessment that said he was measuring Walker against some invisible scale. My stomach knotted instinctively. I wanted this to go well, needed it to, even, and I felt a flicker of protectiveness rise in my chest. Walker didn't deserve to be judged, not after everything.

"Connor, this is Walker," I said, gesturing between them. "Walker, my brother."

"Nice to meet you," Walker said, extending his hand. Connor shook it firmly, their hands lingering a little longer than necessary in that silent communication guys seemed to understand instinctively.

"Good to meet you too," Connor said. "I've heard a lot about you."

"Yeah? All good, I hope."

"Mostly," Connor said with a grin, and I could feel Walker relax a little.

Connor tilted his head slightly. "Walker Hannan, hockey's bad boy with a temper? Some of the stuff on the forums, what I've seen in the game, the guy you beat up, just saying… "

Walker didn't even blink. "I know you don't have to take my word for it, but I'm… different now… with Finn. He makes me… " He dipped his head. "Kinder, to myself and… yeah… "

Connor held his gaze for a beat longer, then nodded. "Good." He took a sip of his drink, then added with a smirk, "You hurt him, and… well, I'll hire three guys to take you down." He glanced at his slim frame and gave a dry chuckle. "Because I sure as hell can't do it myself."

"If I hurt Finn, I'll stand there and let you wail on me as much as you want." He tugged at my hand and laced our fingers. "I love your brother, and I would never hurt him."

Connor nodded. "Noted." Then, he made a hand gesture with two fingers to his eyes and pointed at Walker, the universal code for watching you.

"Jesus, Con," I grumped, and Connor and Walker both snorted laughs. Assholes.

Moments later, Harper appeared all smiles and energy, her dark hair falling loose over her shoulders. "Sorry I'm late! Work ran over."

"You're fine, Sprite," Walker assured her, hugging her hard. "Harper, this is my man, Finn."

My man... my skin heated, and I felt all squirrely inside. How did this man have such power to make me feel wanted?

"Hi. Nice to meet you." I greeted her with a warm hug. She looked like a mini-Walker, with the same dark eyes and stubborn tilt to her chin. As for her smile... yeah, pure Walker.

She turned to me once we'd all settled, her eyes twinkling. "So, Finn, you're the guy who's got my brother acting like a soft puppy instead of a raging defenseman. I gotta say, I didn't think it was possible."

I laughed. "I'll take that as a compliment."

"You should. He's not easy, you know. All gruff and silent treatment, mood swings, and loyalty issues."

"Yeah," I said with a smirk. "And that's just before breakfast."

She snorted. "You're good. You'll need that quick wit to keep up with him."

"I'm learning. Slowly."

Her tone softened then, more sincere. "He's been through a lot. And I've never seen him... like this. He looks at you like you're the only person in the room."

I felt my throat tighten. "He means everything to me."

She nodded, reaching over to touch my arm. "Then, we're good."

With introductions done, we ordered drinks and food, and we laughed and joked through dinner. I watched as Harper's gaze lingered on Connor. Her usual animated chatter slowed slightly, her smile softening whenever he spoke. Connor, too, seemed to sit a little straighter, glancing her way more often than he probably realized.

By the time our dinners arrived, they were both practically glowing. Harper laughed a little too loud at one of Connor's jokes, and Connor kept asking questions about her job, looking genuinely interested in every answer. Walker caught my eye from across the table and smirked.

I nudged his knee under the table. "They're either

falling in love or plotting world domination," I acknowledged.

"Could be both," Walker replied, grin widening.

Dinner flowed easily, conversation bouncing between the four of us. Walker recounted one of Bob's infamous locker room pranks, and Harper chimed in with a story about her gym mishaps that had Connor practically crying with laughter. Each time Harper spoke, Connor's gaze softened. Each time Connor cracked a joke, Harper's smile widened slightly more.

I felt a warm, steady feeling in my chest that I hadn't expected. This wasn't just dinner. This wasn't just a date. This felt like family.

Connor set down his fork and leaned back in his chair, giving Walker a curious look. "Hey, you hear about Lemanski?"

Walker frowned. "What about him?" I didn't know who Lemanski was, but how Walker stiffened made me think this was a bad thing to discuss. Or a good thing? Who knew?

Connor leaned forward. "Something about a knee operation and the Vipers putting him out for an op?"

Walker blinked. "Seriously? You know more than me then. Are you sure? He just came back from injury."

Ah, so Lemanski was a New York Vipers player. Why did Walker look so weird right now, glancing at me and trying to smile? Shit. Was this an injury where maybe they'd want to call up Walker to replace him? My chest tightened.

Connor nodded. "The forums are churning hard. D-man down. Does that mean you'll get called up?"

Fuck. I was right.

Walker laughed, but it sounded short and dry. "There are far better and more level-headed replacements than me to head to the Big Apple." He reached for my hand under the table and squeezed it. "I'm not going anywhere."

By the time dessert arrived, the tension in my chest had shifted. Not from nerves or anxiety but from the realization of how easily Walker had slipped into my life. Like he'd always been there... like he belonged.

And that's what scared me most. Even as he smiled at me and pretended the news about this Lemanski guy hadn't shocked him, I couldn't help but wonder... what happens when New York calls him back?

SEVENTEEN

Walker

IN THE PARKING LOT AFTER DINNER WITH THE SIBS, WE all decided to head to different places. Harper had hinted strongly that she and Connor would like to continue the evening at our apartment, and me being the best older brother ever, told her to rock that roll. I took Finn by the hand with a final wave and warning to always use protection because I wasn't ready to be an uncle yet and led my man to my truck. Tiny flakes blew around us, crystals that danced about in the lights, making the cramped lot come alive.

"Kind of like a Disney movie," I commented as I dug in my front pocket for my keys. "One of us should start singing about letting shit go."

"I'm pretty sure the word shit was not in that

song," Finn replied as his hold on my hand tightened. I smirked and looked at my pocket like I could see through the cotton material to see my keys within, a la Clark Kent, to find Finn staring at our hands.

"Hey." I gave his hand a shake. His gaze flew to my face. "You okay?"

"Yes, of course. Just a little tired." He plastered on a smile that didn't quite reach those pretty eyes of his, but I let it go. I suspected he was feeling his feels about a possible call-up to New York. I'd opted out of that worry for now. Just shoved it aside. Either the Vipers would call me back or they wouldn't. There was nothing I could do either way. I wasn't going to fight being called back to the pros. That was the end goal after all. Or it had been when I'd gotten here. Still was. Wasn't it? Shit. I didn't even know anymore. No need to borrow worry as Dr. Quackers liked to toss out over funky tea and goatee strokes.

"When we get to your place, I'll rub your feet." I kissed him on his furrowed brow and opened the car door for him. I was a gentleman after all. And if anyone said otherwise, I would punch them in the face. Mentally. Mental face punches were allowed. Possibly. Maybe not. I'd have to talk to Doc Quackers about that...

"That sounds perfect." He rose up onto his toes to kiss me on the lips. Just a little peck, but it held a lot of hidden promise.

We rode along in comfortable companionship. Finn made conversation about the weather, the meal, and our siblings, anything but the big old elephant in the back seat.

That was fine with me. Once we were inside his place, he barely had his shoes off before he launched himself at me. With one arm in my coat, and the other out, I hurried to throw my arms around him as he locked his legs around my waist. His mouth slammed over mine. I took a step back to find the wall as his fingers carded into my hair, his tongue sliding into my mouth. He was rock hard against my belly. Wobbling slightly, I cupped his pert ass as I met his kiss with equal hunger.

"Take me to bed," he panted when we broke for air.

"Sure, yeah," I mumbled, hoisting him higher and carrying him to his bedroom. He sucked on my throat the entire way to his bed, nipping lightly, then suckling hard. Marking me, I was sure. It was more than a little hot. We fell into his bed. He pushed me onto my back, rolling over to straddle me as he pawed at the buttons on my shirt. One flew across the room. I lay back; my hands linked behind my head and let him have his way. He had me stripped down in no time, his lips moving over me, leaving hot, moist trails as he tried to taste every damn inch of me before he gave the head of my cock a hot kiss.

"Finn, honey, that is amazing," I groaned out. He took just the fat head between his lips. Next, he rolled my balls around in his warm palm. I fisted the sheets as he blew me. Just when the sensations were getting to be too much, he pulled off, lips pink and wet, pupils blown, and sat back on his heels still fully dressed.

"Can I ride you?"

As if any sane man would refuse that request. "Yeah, but are you sure you don't want to—"

"I want you inside me now." He yanked his clothes off as if we were racing a clock. Maybe inside his head we were. "I'm negative and on PrEP." My eyes moved down to his lovely cock as he spoke while fumbling about on the nightstand. I longed to take it into my mouth, but it seemed the world's best teacher had other plans for it. Maybe later. This was fully Finn's moment to direct. He produced a tube of lube and flicked the lid with one brow raised. Oh right. I had to make words now.

Talking was hard with this wiry, wonderful man sitting on my thighs stark naked. He was perfection. Slim but tone, with subtle wisps of hair on his chest and thighs.

"Same, shit... " I grunted when he poured a generous amount of lube on my cock. "Shit... Finn baby... shit." His hand circled my cock, working the lube to coat my length before he reached around to press some slick into his hole. "Next round, you sit on my face, okay?" I needed to taste his tight-furled opening. Only it wouldn't be tight when he was done bouncing up and down on my dick. It would be loose and wet with my cum, which was not at all a turnoff of any kind.

"Yeah, yeah, yeah," he panted as he fingered himself. My cock was oozing precum, my breath hitching up as I watched him ready himself for me. With a small shudder, he removed his fingers, splayed his palms on my pecs, and gazed down at me with hot, black eyes. No hazel remained now. "Hold your dick in place."

I shoved my hand down to fist my cock. He moved up on his knees an inch or so, then sat down on my prick. One slow, tight, warm inch at a time, he lowered himself downward. His fingers bit into my chest, nails digging into the flesh. I couldn't have cared less. He was free to peel me out of my skin as long as he kept his tight ass around my dick.

"Oh my God… " His words were ground out as his body stretched around me.

"Fucking hell… so tight," I coughed out. I wanted desperately to thrust up, but I was not the man in charge. Finn was. When he was ready, he would move. That took a moment, and then his hips began to roll. His head fell back. His mouth opened. And he clenched. "Fuck!" I'd not be able to bite back my orgasm if he kept doing that.

"You like it when my ass hugs your cock?"

"Jesus, baby, who knew teachers talked so dirty?" I gave my ass muscles a little flex. My cock moved up just a wee bit. His eyes flared.

"We have… lots of words… do that again. Harder. I want to feel you for days," he growled down at me, nostrils flared and brow dotted with sweat.

"You sure?"

He lowered his lips to mine and ravaged my mouth. The kiss was all teeth and tongue, primal, wet and sloppy and fucking divine. I dug my heels into the mattress, then pushed up into an ugly bridge pose. Finn lost his shit. He arched like a cat, yowled like one too, and began to bounce up and down with vigor. All I could do was hold on to his hips, so he didn't fling himself off my dick to the floor, and enjoy myself. Which I did and then some. He fucked me hard, his tiny ass smacking down on my thighs over and over until my balls drew up.

"Here it comes," I ground out, pushing up higher, driving my cock into him. His eyes rolled back when I grabbed his bouncing dick to stroke it. Cum flew out of him, strings of hot white pearls that dotted my chest and chin. My dick pulsed with my release, filling him as his body milked mine. He rose and fell for another solid minute, his prick oozing cum with each slap of skin to skin.

"Good… that's sooo good," he gasped. I released his dick, and he fell on top of me, his nose buried in my throat, my cock nestled sweetly in his ass. I massaged his glutes, pressing them together then spreading them wide, imagining my spunk oozing out of his ass. A shiver ran over him, so I released his cheeks and turned my head to kiss his damp hair.

"Okay, baby?" I asked as I gently tried to ease him off me to the side. We both moaned when my soft dick slipped out of him, my cock leaving a wet streak on his taint. He was an overcooked noodle at that point, so he simply lay where he landed on the bedding, face in a pillow, arms at his sides.

"So okay." He sighed into the pillow. I smiled

proudly. Sure, he had done all the work, but my dick had reduced him to linguine.

"Excellent. Rest. I'm going to get us a cloth," I whispered and kissed his shoulder.

A sigh was his reply. I rolled out of the tangled bedding to make my way into the tiny bathroom. I washed up and re-wet and wrung out a dark green washcloth before pattering back to my lover. He hadn't moved an inch. His shoulders rose and fell with a slow, steady motion that made me think he was asleep. When I knelt on the bed, he stirred.

"Going to clean you up," I whispered, and he spread his legs a little wider. I gently rubbed the cloth over his tender hole as he mumbled something into the pillow. "You want some water or something to eat?"

"No," he softly replied, waving a hand about over his head. "Just want you to spoon me."

I whipped the wet cloth over my shoulder. He wiggled close when I slid under the blanket, the messy sheets balled up under us. I curled into his back, placed my palm on his belly, and breathed in the intoxicating smell of me, Finn, and sex.

"I hope you don't have to go back," he said sleepily.

I hoped not as well—mostly maybe—but that was

out of my hands. And for now, this night, it was out of my head. Nothing existed but me and my lover.

———

MORNING ARRIVED WITH A FLURRY OF NOTIFICATIONS, sending my cell into a buzzing frenzy. Not since I'd been ten and poked at a hornet's nest with a hockey stick had I heard such a steady drone. Thankfully, my phone couldn't sting. The hornet's nest was one of those life lessons we hear so much about.

Finn was snoring softly beside me, one leg out of the covers, his back bared to my sight. I bent down to place a kiss on that soft spot between his shoulder blades. He didn't move. I did it again before wriggling the cover out from under me to cover him fully. I sat up, bleary-eyed, and picked up my phone.

There was a slew of messages that grabbed my eye, the first being a text from Harper with a meme of Bob Kelso from *Scrubs* with two thumbs up, both pointing at himself, reading, "Who got laid last night?"

I snort laughed. Finn mumbled something about corn dogs. Smiling to myself, I rose, found my pants lying on the floor, and stepped into them. With my phone in my hand, I replied to my sister with a GIF of

Blanche from *Golden Girls* that had ME TOO, GIRL on the bottom. I took a piss, washed my hands, and went in search of caffeine.

The kitchen was bathed in morning light, wintry and dull, as the sun was partially hidden behind snow clouds. I made my way to the coffee machine, started a pot, and went to stand on a round red throw rug in front of the sink to keep my bare feet off the cold linoleum.

Knowing I couldn't pretend not to have seen the notice from the Vipers, I decided to deal with that first. The other texts from the art guys and a few dozen notifications from various hockey sites would wait. If this message from the GM in New York was what I thought it was going to be, the news lighting up my phone would be moot.

In typical Mike Gallows' fashion, the call-up was short, sweet, and to the point. I was to report to the team today and be ready to play tonight. JFC. That wasn't enough time to say goodbye to Finn and my sister and grab some clean underwear.

My phone read ten a.m., so yeah, time was ticking. A tiny thrill ran through me at the thought of being back in the Big Apple. Obviously, the Vipers had spoken to the head coach here and had gotten a good report about my progress with my off-ice issues.

We all knew that on the ice, I was a fucking legend. Not my words, the words of my fave sports writer in NYC. If I could show the team that I was in control of my anger, this little callback might turn into a permanent spot on the roster. Stranger things had happened. I could very well be helping the Vipers secure a playoff berth if I kept my nose clean. Nothing was more damn exciting than playing to win the cup.

I was smiling when I heard a soft cough in the doorway. Glancing up from my cell, I saw Finn leaning on the doorframe, wearing one of my oversized Viper jerseys, fleece pants, and a fresh-out-of-bed tousled well-loved look that made me want to toss him right back into bed to rumple him a bit more.

"You look happy." And the smile fell from my face. "No, hey, don't do that."

Looking into his sad brown-green eyes, most of the joy I'd felt about being called back faded with the sunlight as sleet began to pepper the window over the sink.

"I won't lie to you." I inhaled deeply, then let it out. "I'm going back to New York. I'm excited to go back, yes, but not excited about leaving you. Is there any way you could come with me?"

He shook his head. I had known it would be a long shot. "I have classes and obligations here."

"Yeah, I know." I tossed my phone onto the counter as sleet and snow whipped in over the lake. "It'll probably just be temporary, babe. Once Lemanski is on the mend… "

He gave me a quirky, sorrowful smile and pushed from the jamb to make his way to the throw rug. "It sounded pretty serious." He reached up to cup my whiskery jaw. "You go play hockey. It's the thing you love most in life."

I put my hand over his and shook my head.

"No, the things I love most in life are you and Harper."

"We love you, too. And we'll be here when you get back."

Such optimism. I admired that about him. "And if I don't come back? Will you come to me?"

I knew Harper would. Or I *had* known. If this thing with Connor got serious, would she move back to Manhattan? She was happy at the gym now, doing what she loved, signing up for bouts around the area. Should I expect her to pick up and trudge after me yet again? Shit. Okay, this call-up was quickly losing some of its initial shine.

"Let's just take it a day at a time and see what happens, okay?"

That was the sensible thing to do. Asking him to uproot his life on a maybe or what-if scenario was inconsiderate. Playing it by ear. Yep, totally mature way to go. I hated being mature at times...

I nodded, turned my face into his palm, and kissed his lifeline. A line that I prayed would include me in it for years to come.

EIGHTEEN

Finn

_____

DAY TWENTY-NINE. FOUR WEEKS AND A DAY. A freaking lifetime, and I felt every second in my bones. My body ached with missing Walker every night I'd gone to bed alone, every time I opened the fridge and saw the stupid chili sauce he liked, or every time I hung up from our daily sitting-in-bed video calls.

He'd been called up to that Buffalo game, and at first, I was too caught up in his excitement and being super supportive—he was finally returning to the show. But then the Vipers had gone on their Canadian swing, nearly two weeks of back-to-back away games, plus extra time for team bonding in Banff. Fuck's sake. I couldn't visit him, between Walker's new schedule and the Vipers being out of town. After twenty-eight days of phone calls and video chats, I couldn't touch him.

And today, finally, I would get to do as much touching as possible.

I stood at the kitchen counter, a half-eaten piece of toast forgotten on my plate, double-checking my backpack for what felt like the hundredth time. Main luggage, already in Bob's car? Check. Walker's spare hoodie for the game? Check. Folded tight at the bottom. Charger, wallet, backup battery, water for the drive? Check.

A ping lit up my phone, then two more in rapid succession.

Walker: Hey sexy, don't be late. You're my good luck charm.

Walker: Ps... I love you xxxx

Walker: PPS... I miss you xxxxxxxxxxx

I grinned like an idiot.

Finn: Leaving now.

Finn: Also... I love you X <3

Finn: And also... I miss you X X X X X

Finn: God, I miss you.

"Ready?" Taft's voice echoed from the hallway. Bob was already in the car, Taft was in charge of organizing me, and both were as overexcited as kids heading to a carnival that they were coming for the one game. Then, they had to be back tomorrow for a showdown against their league rivals. On the other hand, I was on day one of spring break, which meant ten days I could stay at Walker's rental apartment and focus solely on loving and touching him and getting a refill of my man. I slung my bag over my shoulder and hurried down to the car.

The drive to New York was all caffeine, banter, and the occasional outburst of hockey trivia of things Taft and Bob thought I needed to know. They weren't as cool as the stats that Chip threw out, but it made me smile, nonetheless.

"Did you know," Taft began, his eyes on the road. "That in 1979, the Erie Egrets went an entire season without a single shorthanded goal? I got that from Chip."

Bob snorted. "Total myth. That stat's been debunked about five times. You're thinking of the Albany Anchors, and it was '81."

"Fake news," Taft shot back, delighted at the chance to argue. "I had a vintage card of their goalie, Ned 'No-Hands' Hansen. Legendary guy. Stopped a puck with his face once and still kept the shutout."

"Yeah, and then, he retired with a broken nose and two chipped teeth. Heroic, sure, but not the best strategy."

I grinned and leaned back, letting the back-and-forth wash over me.

"Also," Bob added smugly. "Walker's playing style? Pure '92 Vultures. Controlled aggression. You can tell he watched those tapes growing up."

"That's not history, that's opinion," Taft muttered, reaching for another handful of trail mix. "But sure. Let the record show Bob's hockey hot takes are alive and well."

They continued bickering for half the drive, trivia flying between them like slapshots. It was ridiculous and completely perfect.

Taft and Bob made it their mission to keep my spirits high, and I appreciated it even if my stomach was twisted in knots the whole way.

We'd barely pulled into the parking structure outside the arena when my phone buzzed again.

Walker: On the ice soon. I'll find you.

Bob clapped a hand on my shoulder. "Let's go see our boy light up the place."

Inside, the energy hit me like a wave. Lights, noise, fans in jerseys shouting over each other, the buzz of the Zamboni still smoothing the ice. It was everything I remembered, magnified by the fact that *this time* Walker was one of the guys skating out.

Bob and Taft got what I jokingly called backstage

passes for the three of us. We didn't end up behind the bench, but our seats were right behind the glass, close enough that I could see the texture of the ice and feel the vibration of each hit. People noticed them: Taft with his shyness and Bob trying to act cool but loving the attention. A couple of kids asked for autographs.

I didn't expect to get noticed, but I caught a couple of nods from people in Walker jerseys, subtle, quick, and maybe they recognized me. Perhaps they didn't. Maybe it was just a fan thing, a number thing. Who knew? But at that moment, I didn't care. I was there. He was on the ice. And in a few hours, I'd be in his arms again. That was all that mattered.

When he came out for warmups, wearing number 10 in NY colors—similar to the Copperheads colors, only bolder—with the black viper on his chest, I couldn't breathe. I didn't yell. Didn't cheer. I stood at the glass, heart hammering, and watched the man I loved take his place among the best.

Twenty-nine days. And there he was.

During warmups, he skated toward our side of the rink and slowed just enough to glance toward the glass for one perfect second. I didn't know if he'd seen me or if it was instinct, but I lifted my hand and pressed it flat to the barrier. And then, he did it too. Walker's glove met the glass opposite mine, a heartbeat of contact, and that was it. That was everything. Every aching day apart, every late-night phone call, every lonely second—worth it.

Before they skated back into the locker room, he came to the glass again, made a heart with his hands, then blew me a freaking kiss.

Fuck my life, I was so gone on this man.

The game started, and the score tilted wildly in New York's favor somewhere between the first faceoff and the end of the second. Pittsburgh looked tired, sluggish, maybe worn from travel. Walker was sharp and solid, no nerves to be seen. The puck came off his stick with a smoothness that made it look effortless. He'd danced around a defenseman, toe-dragged it like poetry, and sent a crisp pass to his linemate, who buried it in the top corner. The crowd erupted, the row behind us jumping to their feet like someone had fired a starting gun. Taft wriggled in excitement beside me, Bob slapped the glass, and I—

I just stood there stunned, grinning, my heart nearly bursting with pride. He looked up toward the glass again, and I was already there, palm against the barrier, breath fogging the surface, just in case he was looking.

He celebrated with the team, all huddled in a mass

of celebration, and then, he deliberately skated by where we sat and nodded with a grin.

"I'm so fucking glad they called him up," someone said from behind me during the second break. "Did you see that pass? "

"Gonna be a regular if they've got sense."

"Doesn't play like he's spent any time in the minors."

"Fucking A!"

I stared down at the bench where Walker sat, breathing hard. Sweat darkened his jersey at the collar, and he leaned forward, watching the second line do their job.

That was *my* Walker they were talking about, and I was so damn proud of him.

And after the game -- after the win -- I'd get to hold him again.

The final horn sounded, and the crowd roared, the noise like thunder through the arena. I stood and clapped until my hands stung, my throat raw from cheering. All I saw was Walker.

Helmet off. Hair soaked with sweat. Grinning like a lunatic as he fist-bumped his teammates, his cheeks flushed with exertion. He looked like he belonged out there, with the speed, the intensity, and the damn glow of it all. But then, his gaze swept the crowd, and everything shifted when it landed on me.

He didn't need to wave. That look said it all.

The post-game chaos was a blur of cheers and fans pouring into the concourse, all of it background noise as I stood frozen just outside the private access door, my pass lanyard clenched in a death grip. Bob and Taft had disappeared somewhere, probably talking hockey with the staff or hitting up concessions for celebratory hot dogs since they were heading back to Rochester tonight.

All I could think about was Walker.

It was a long forty minutes before he was out, but when he exited, his hair still damp from the shower and dressed in his suit, he was sex personified. It wasn't until his eyes landed on me that I swear the world stilled.

"Finn."

He said it like a prayer, pulling me into him.

I didn't care if people were watching. I wrapped my arms around him so tightly it might have bruised him, my face pressed to the curve of his neck, and I breathed him in.

"Jesus," he whispered into my hair. "I missed you so much. Every night. Every morning. Every second."

I nodded, words locked behind the lump in my throat. "Same. All of it."

He leaned in, his lips brushing mine in a kiss that wasn't hurried or heated—it was home. Slow and sure.

"Fans were talking about you in the stands. Said you should stay up. Said you had presence."

Walker's breath hitched. "Yeah?" He sounded so damn torn, but if this was where my man was playing, and I wanted to be with him, then maybe it was on me to move to New York.

"Yeah," I said, smiling. "But I already knew that."

He laughed, a low, breathless sound that shook between us. "Did you pack for ten days?"

"Of course. Taft and Bob left it with the team."

"Then we'd better get moving. I plan to spend every minute I can making up for the last twenty-nine."

THE CALL CAME AS WE SAT IN A CAFÉ NEAR THE Bethesda Fountain in Central Park, sharing a cinnamon bun and drinking overpriced lattes from paper cups that steamed in the chill air.

When my phone buzzed with Detective Aster's

number, Walker was halfway through a story about one of his teammates getting pranked with shaving cream. I'd been dreading this call, knowing it would mean I'd have to go to court, that it would stir up everything again and put little Jamie in the spotlight. I hesitated, then answered.

"Detective?"

Walker stiffened and placed a hand on mine.

"He pleaded guilty." His voice was steady, a low rumble of professionalism edged with something softer, relief maybe, or fatigue.

I blinked. "Wait—he did?"

"Yeah. No trial. No drawn-out legal process. The DA struck a deal. A guilty plea on all counts. He'll serve a full sentence. No parole until after the minimum term is up. It's solid. No room for appeal."

"What does that mean for Walker and me?" I asked quietly.

"You're clear. Both of you. No depositions, no testimony, no appearances. You're officially disconnected from the case unless something radically changes, which I don't expect."

He paused, then added, "You did good, Finn. You and Walker both. You stepped in when it counted. I hope, now, you can both put this behind you."

When I hung up, Walker watched me carefully. "Finn?"

"Jamie's dad pleaded guilty," I said, still trying to process the words. "There won't be a trial. No testimony. It's... done."

Walker leaned back in his chair, quiet for a moment. Then, he reached across the table and took my hand. "That's good, right? No more dragging it out for Jamie? For his mom?"

I nodded slowly. "Yeah. I think so. It just... feels sudden."

He squeezed my fingers. "But it's done." He scooted around to sit next to me, pulling me close. I buried my face in his neck, inhaling his scent.

"I love you." I kissed him soundly to underscore the point. "I love you."

We stayed like that for a while, and the world kept moving. He was still in New York, I was in Rochester, but for a moment, none of that mattered.

Eventually, he pressed a kiss to my temple. "You okay?"

I nodded into his shoulder. "I will be."

NINETEEN

Walker

WE ONLY HAD TWO DAYS LEFT TOGETHER.

I was trying my best to focus on the good and not the upsetting, as Dr. Quackers had suggested I do in our biweekly call last night. As I rounded the corner of 40th Street and 6th Avenue, sweat in my eyes and my hamstrings protesting the long jog, I was finding it difficult to fixate on anything good about only having two days left with Finn. I slowed, breathless, and worked to catch my breath at the 6th Avenue entrance to Bryant Park. My temporary lodgings were just a few blocks away, and I had quickly fallen back in love with this charming slice of green amid the chaotic concrete jungle. Well, it would be green soon. Right now, it was cold and dull, the snow that had fallen a few days ago now dirty brown. But soon, when February melted away and March arrived with the St. Patty's Day parade, this little chunk of property by the famous library would be alive with flowers, birds, and concerts.

I looked forward to that because I'd need all of those things to keep my mind off how much I was going to be missing my man.

Panting like a mule, I checked my mileage on my smartwatch and saw that I was done for the day. A relief, to be sure. Running was fun, I guess. What was even more fun was darting across the street to this tiny brioche shop to buy sweet treats for me and my sleepy boyfriend.

After my purchase, I made my way back to Bryant Park, cutting through the snowy green to check on my reservations at the grill/restaurant only to find that it was closed. Which, yeah, doh! Walker, it was seven in the morning. Even this early, the rest of the city was hopping. Life never slowed in the Big Apple. I studied the restaurant's green canopy while a few bold pigeons bobbed around me, eyeballing my white bag. I made a mental note to text the restaurant later to check on our dinner reservation for this evening. Finn would be back in Rochester before

Valentine's Day arrived in five days, so we were doing the fancy romantic dinner tonight.

Turning from the eatery, I nearly ran into a thin dude whom I instantly recognized. The twink phone thief from last fall. He looked healthier than he had the last time we'd seen each other. I took a step back since I wasn't sure if I should be talking to him because there was litigation pending.

"Hey, no, I'm not here to hassle you," he hurried to say, hands up, palms out. He was wrapped up in a dark coat, his face free of makeup, his hair now dark red, cut short. A plush purple winter coat with gold buttons as big as the brioches in my bag was the only sign of his usual brash fashion choices. "I thought it was you. I was over there." He waved a manicured hand at the now silent carousel. "I like to come here to look at it before I go to work at the rink."

"Uh-huh." I lowered my shoulders a touch. "Why would you want to talk to me?"

"Oh, well, I just… " His exhalation was long. It clouded in front of him and, then, dissipated. "I wanted to let you know that I'm dropping the assault charges." No shit. Okay. Well, that was good news. "I've been in rehab on and off. Just did another thirty days to kick ketamine. It sucked." A sad laugh bubbled out of him. I said nothing. "We talked a lot." He looked squeamish, nervous.

"Uh-huh. Yeah, I talked a lot to a counselor, too. Anger shit. Look." I glanced skyward and, then, back at the skinny kid. And he was a kid. Maybe twenty if that. Pretty, even without the makeup, but washed out too, if that made sense. Addiction will do that to a person. "I shouldn't have hit you."

"No, hey, no, you should have. I mean, maybe not so many times, but yeah, I was asking for it. I stole your phone. I was going to get you alone and probably steal your wallet as well. For K. Ketamine."

"Yeah, right, I know the slang."

"Sure, yeah, well, therapy has these rules, and one of them is to apologize to someone that you've wronged, right?" I nodded. Dr. Quackers and I had discussed that a few times, and he had encouraged me to do just that if I ever got the chance. I'd assumed this guy would wring me out in court, and rightfully so, but now it looked like we both had some amends to make. "So, I just wanted to say that I'm sorry for being such a little bitch. I shouldn't have led you on or stolen your phone or planned to lift your wallet when we reached a motel."

"Nah, hey, you were in a bad place. I was too. I shouldn't have reacted like I did. With fists. That's totally on me. I'd be happy to pay for your medical bills."

"No, that's fine. My father works at the rink too, so his insurance covered it. And since I got clean, he took me back and got me this job."

"Cool, good, that's good. I'm glad life is working out for you, Kyle." He appeared surprised that I recalled his name. As if I could forget it splashed on all those court papers.

"Same. Same." He offered me his hand. I took it. We shook, just once, then our hands fell back to our sides. "I'm going to call my attorney today. I think we both need to just move past our dumb mistakes, yeah?"

"Yeah, I agree."

"Cool. Okay, well, saw you in the media, that school stuff."

"Yeah."

"Cool."

"Okay."

"Anyway, I better get to work. Those skates don't sharpen themselves. I hope things go well for you. Thank you for accepting my apology." He gave me a shy smile.

"Thanks for accepting mine."

He nodded before jogging off toward the small

rink. I stood there for a few minutes, then I unclenched my fingers from the brioche bag so that I could text my lawyer to fill him in on this random meeting with Kyle. My attorney was pleased to hear that things had sorted themselves out and ended our conversation with a plea to keep myself out of trouble. I was reasonably sure I could probably do that. With the help of a good therapist and the love of a good man.

I headed home to deliver brioche—and a few dozen kisses—to that good man still snoozing in my bed.

I was going to make the most of these last two cold February days.

MARCH 4. A PRETTY COMMON DAY. NOTHING THAT would live in infamy unless you were a professional hockey player.

This year the trade deadline was March 4, and I awoke to pings on my phone. Rolling over to pat Finn's side of the bed and finding it cold made me grumbly. Moving to my other side to find my phone to see that there were rumblings out of St. Louis that Manny Milchan was on the block made me more grumbly. Rumors were saying that his wife, a model from Queens, was desperate to move back into the five boroughs. Lying on my back watching the pundits making educated—and sometimes not educated at all—guesses about whether one of the league's best defensemen would be coming to the Vipers was icky.

Seriously, I could not think of a better word. It was icky, and it left a bad taste in my mouth that was even worse than my garlic morning breath. If they bought out Milchan, I was for sure on the next plane back to Rochester or, even worse, headed further from Finn.

Eyes bleary with sleep still, I dug around inside my chest to see if I could find some disappointment. Oh yeah, there it was, right under my heart. It sucked monkey testes that a guy who had worked so fucking hard to figure himself out, and had given 100 percent to the team, would be tossed out the window like a mismatched sock. But that was professional sports. One day you were the golden child, and the next you were a tarnished tin can being kicked down the road. And while I was feeling a little hurt over being mentioned repeatedly as said tin can, on the other hand, being sent back down meant being sent back to Finn's arms.

Reading over the tidbits as I knocked back a power shake before my morning run, the initial upset was slowly fading into acceptance mixed with some real joy. Not at all what a pro player should be feeling at the moment his career takes yet another nose dive, but there it was.

Sipping my shake, I rang Finn, not texted, because I needed to hear his voice.

"Hey, you," he said after picking up on the second ring. Teachers did have to get up and at them early after all.

"Hey back," I said, leaning on the counter, phone to one ear, my shake in the other. I began swirling the thick chocolate protein shake. "So, there are rumors…"

I heard him exhale softly. "Bad rumors or good rumors?"

"Depends on your perspective." I took a swig, swallowed, and walked to my slider glass door. The patio was bare of any kind of outdoor furniture. Far below, taxis slipped in and out of traffic. People were filling the sidewalks. Charter buses were already squeezing through side streets to drop off tourists. "I think they're going to cut a deal with Milchan. He's a big name in the league, won the Norris Trophy four times."

"Wow." He had no clue what the Norris Trophy was, bless his heart, but he was being a good hockey boyfriend.

"Yeah, so he's looking to get out of St. Louis. I think the Vipers are going to bring him to New York as a permanent replacement for Lemanski." Small bits of flotsam floated on the top of my shake. "Which is totally a killer move if they can swing it with the cap situation they have. He's a legend."

"But still, that's shitty. You've been working so hard and playing so well."

"Yeah well, that's hockey." I sighed before taking another sip of what was a pretty chalky damn drink if I did say so myself. I did not like this new powder that I'd bought. "So, just to let you know what may happen. They might swap me and some other less than stellar players flat out for Milchan or, and this is what I hope happens, they send me back down."

There was a long pause as he sorted that info out. "So you think it's either St. Louis or Rochester. But they may keep you to play with this Milchan, right?"

"Nah, not enough in the cap to finagle that. They'll ship me somewhere, bet your tasty ass on it, and I hope it's back to you."

"I hope so too. I miss you. I hate that they're treating you players like possessions."

"That's pretty much what we are." My phone vibrated with a call. I scrolled it up and saw Gallows' name come up. Okay, yeah, this was a call from the GM. "Hey, the GM is ringing me up. At seven-ten in the morning. I need to take this."

"Yes, please take it. Call me when you know something. I love you. Everything will work out."

"Love you too." I ended one call to take the other. Mike was gracious, wired on coffee I was sure, so he was passing along his praise way too quickly. Understanding all his preliminary toe-dancing about my improvement in all areas as well as my dedication to the organization didn't need to be understood, I knew where the head pats were leading. When he informed me that I was being shipped back to Rochester for more development, I thanked him. And I mean, I thanked him sincerely, something he seemed to be shocked about but took in stride.

When we said our goodbyes, I took a moment to knock back my shake, grimace, and then, whisper goodbye to Manhattan. Then, I called my man.

He answered on the first ring. Hell, maybe it was a half ring. That amused me.

"Walker," he whispered as if we were discussing war plans on a secret line. "What did the GM say? I'm crossing my eyes and toes and fingers."

"Hope you have room in your bathroom for my toothbrush again," I told him. "I'm coming home."

Home. Yep, that was the proper word. They say home is where the heart is, and mine was in Rochester with a certain world's best teacher.

Epilogue

FINN

Eight months later, November

OUR HOUSEWARMING HAD QUICKLY TURNED INTO A full-on Copperheads party. Walker and I had deliberately invested his money from before he was sent down the first time into this sprawling place near Rochester for moments just like this. A perfect balance of privacy and community. My commute to school was an easy forty-five minutes, close enough for comfort, yet far enough to avoid awkward encounters with parents in the grocery store aisles. The house was everything we'd dreamed, spacious enough for Walker to host the entire team comfortably and for me to finally have my own art studio tucked into the attic, complete with wide windows overlooking a lake. The studio quickly became my sanctuary, a place of light, color, and quiet.

Tonight, though, was anything but quiet. The house buzzed with laughter and chatter, teammates spilling from the kitchen into the living room and even out onto the back porch. Walker stood by the kitchen island, relaxed and smiling, the new captain of the Copperheads. The leadership suited him, and confidence radiated from him as he helped build the team into something truly special.

The art guys—Chip, Taft, Arnaud, and Bob— were scattered throughout the crowd. Harper and Connor had long since disappeared somewhere, and their easy love warmed something deep in my chest. Family mingled with friends, blurring into a single vibrant picture of the life we'd built together.

A sudden eruption of noise from the garden drew everyone's attention, and Walker and I crossed to the window. Through the sliding glass doors, I spotted Bob waving his hands wildly at Arnaud, who was both amused and indignant. Their argument had started inside, innocently enough with chirping, when Bob jokingly called Arnaud a sieve in their last game, an insult no goalie could tolerate. Arnaud's response was a quick and pointed stream of French I couldn't follow, which launched Bob into orbit, and they headed outside to talk, and now what the hell was going on?

"Anyone catch what he said?" Walker asked, slipping his arm around my waist as we watched the unfolding drama.

"No idea," I replied. "But Bob looks ready to explode."

"Bob always looks ready to explode." Taft sighed, coming up beside us with a fresh beer in his hand.

Chip joined us. "Did you know that statistically, team arguments result in a 4.3 percent decrease in pass accuracy during games? Last season, Miller and Andrews argued about sock thickness for thirty-seven minutes, and the team's subsequent game accuracy dropped by exactly that amount. I documented it."

We all stared at Chip, who blinked at us steadily. "What?"

"Standard deviation of 0.5 percent," Chip added.

"Wow, 4.3 percent?" Walker frowned. He took having the C on his chest very seriously. "I need to fix this."

"How do you plan on fixing that?" Taft snorted and waved at the two men under the patio heater, Bob shoving Arnaud and our flexible goalie ducking under his arm. Bob was apoplectic, Arnaud was grinning, and they were wrestling like a couple of kids.

"Should I break it up?" Walker asked.

"No!" we all chorused—no one got in between those two when they started to bicker.

Chip tilted his head slightly. "Did you know the Otters had an 8.6 percent increase in penalties last season because of unresolved sexual tension between teammates Nelson and Ferreira? Statistically significant."

"Huh?" Taft sounded shocked.

"The fuck?" Walker said, wide-eyed, mouth dropping open. The four of us stood at the window, Chip nodding.

"Well, that explains a lot," Taft finally offered.

"Wow, 8.6 percent," Chip repeated. "I need carrots." He then wandered off, leaving Walker, Taft, and me at the window, staring at Bob and Arnaud, who were now pushing, shoving, and shouting. Hell, even Arnaud was shouting now, and that was dangerous. They gave each other one last shove, and then Bob stormed toward the back door and we all pretended not to watch at all.

The back door slammed open. "Do something before I kill him!" Bob shouted at Walker as he passed us. "I'm going home!" He began to storm away but, then, he stopped, came back to me and pressed a kiss on my head. "Great party, Finn. Sorry."

He left then, the front door slamming as dramatically as he'd opened the back.

Arnaud sauntered in as though he weren't angry, but he was red-cheeked and still muttering fiercely in French. The only words I caught clearly were something about "an angry bear needing his claws clipped," which made absolutely no sense to any of us. When he headed over to the fridge for another drink, none of us dared ask what he meant. Some things were best left unexplained, especially with irate French-Canadian goalies.

"I'll fix it," Walker said. "Make them ride the bus together for every away game."

"Yeah, that'll work," Taft deadpanned, then shrugged when Walker scowled at him. "Worth a try, I guess. Beer?"

I waved my half-full bottle, and Walker shook his head.

I leaned into his warmth, breathing in the moment. "You'll fix it," I reassured him, as he started to look worried.

And I had no doubt he would fix things. We'd come so far, each of us separately and together, building something real, something lasting. And standing there, surrounded by our family and friends, I knew it was exactly where I was meant to be.

Home.

With Walker.

"Love you," I whispered, rising onto my toes to brush my lips softly against his, determined to chase away the lingering worry from his eyes. Walker cupped my face gently, deepening the kiss until the world around us faded into warmth and comfort. We only pulled apart when the laughter, cheers, and exaggerated wolf whistles from our friends became impossible to ignore.

"Love you more," he murmured against my lips, eyes twinkling with a promise that went deeper than words.

"Impossible," I said softly.

"I can prove it," Walker said with a playful raise of his eyebrow.

"Yeah?" I teased back, unable to suppress my grin.

Walker turned dramatically toward our family and friends. "Party's over! Everyone out, now!"

Amid the laughter, protests, and good-natured teasing, our guests slowly dispersed, leaving the house quiet and just ours. And once the last car pulled away, Walker showed me exactly how much he loved me.

Twice.

Spectrum and Smoke

One firefighter. One hockey player. One slow burn that had nothing to do with the fire.

Russell "Chip" Cornish has always been the heart of the Rochester Copperheads—he reads the ice in angles and probabilities, and the rest of the world the same way. He keeps his routines, maps every room in steps and distances, and lets his assistance dog Sable do the emotional heavy lifting when the world gets too loud. Then a fire changes everything, and the firefighter who pulls them both from danger turns out to be the one thing Chip can't calculate his way out of.

Pulling a stranger and his dog from a fire was just the job. Dane Rourke hadn't counted on the stranger being quite so impossible to forget—or on breaking every rule he'd signed up for about getting involved. After a second encounter crackles with something neither of them planned for, they start finding reasons to be in the same room—and then the same apartment. Slow and steady, careful and quiet, keeping it hidden from Dane's station captain while a homophobic colleague watches for cracks.

As the Copperheads chase the Cup and Chip and Dane navigate trust and the terrifying leap from careful to committed, they're learning that showing up —every time, even when it's hard—is everything.

Spectrum & Smoke is a steamy, slow-burn MM hockey romance featuring neurodivergent rep, an assistance dog who steals scenes, opposites attract, a hero learning to let someone in, and a love story that goes all the way to Game Seven.

Hockey Series' from RJ Scott & V.L. Locey

Harrisburg Railers

Owatonna U Hockey

Arizona Raptors

Boston Rebels

LA Storm

Chesterford Coyotes - Young Adult

Railers Legacy

Rochester Copperheads

Oxford Knights (coming 2027)

Harrisburg Railers

When hockey wunderkind Tennant Rowe meets his new coach, he knows he's in trouble. Jared Madsen is nine years older than Tennant, impossibly attractive, and — worst of all — his brother's off-limits best friend. Is their chemistry worth the risk?

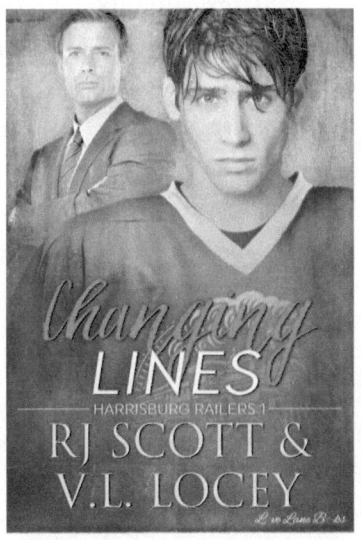

Changing Lines (Railers 1)

Can Tennant show Jared that age is just a number, and that love is all that matters?

The Rowe Brothers are famous hockey hotshots, but as the youngest of the trio, Tennant has always had to play against his brothers' reputations. To get out of their shadows, and against their advice, he accepts a trade to the Harrisburg Railers, where he runs into Jared Madsen. Mads is an old family friend and his brother's one-time teammate. Mads is Tennant's new coach. And Mads is the sexiest thing he's ever laid eyes on.

Jared Madsen's hockey career was cut short by a fault in his heart, but coaching keeps him close to the game. When Ten is traded to the team, his carefully organized world is thrown into chaos. Nine years his junior and his best friend's brother, he knows Ten is strictly off-limits, but as soon as he sees Ten's moves, on and off the ice, he knows that his heart could get him into trouble again.

Harrisburg Railers (Hockey Romance)

1. Changing Lines
2. First Season
3. Deep Edge
4. Poke Check
5. Last Defense
6. Goal Line
7. Neutral Zone
8. Hat Trick

Railers Volume 1 | Railers Volume 2 | Railers Volume 3 | Railers Volume 4

Meet the men of Owatonna University's hockey team

Ryker (Owatonna U, 1)

Ryker is hockey royalty, Jacob is a poor country boy. Can two vastly different people find common ground and become the men they want to be?

Ryker comes from a long line of championship-winning hockey players. Playing college hockey to develop his game is his only focus, and nothing will stand in the way of him working to become the best player. He has no room for relationships, people who point out his flaws, or anyone who calls him on his dreams. He certainly has no place for love, and meeting Jacob is nothing but a useful distraction on the side. After all trying to get his Owatonna Eagles teammate into bed is less work and more play. When tragedy rocks his family, his charmed life crumbles, and the only person he can turn to is the same one who claims to hate him.

Jacob Benson has only known hard work and stifling conservative values his whole life. Born and raised in the small rural community of Eden Crossing, Minnesota, he's the only son of a hard-working but struggling dairy farming family. Jacob is using his skills in hockey to finance his way to an agricultural science degree. These four years at Owatonna U. will probably be the only time he has to enjoy life, gain acceptance about his sexuality, and live openly before his inevitable return to the farm. Running into a pretty rich boy like Ryker Madsen is putting a damper on his enjoyment of life away from home. Ryker's flip, conceited, carefree attitude grates on Jacob's every nerve. So why, if Ryker is everything he dislikes, does he want nothing more than to explore the sinful dreams that his annoying teammate stars in every night?

Ryker

Owatonna U Hockey (Hockey Romance)

1. Ryker
2. Scott
3. Benoit
4. Christmas Lights
5. Valentine's Hearts
6. Desert Dreams

Arizona Raptors

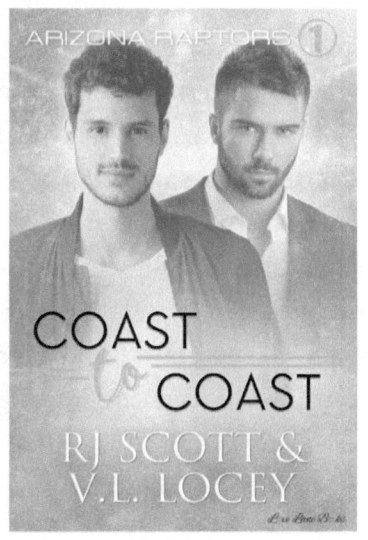

Coast to Coast (Arizona Raptors 1)

Coast To Coast

When opposites attract, this bottom-of-the-league team will never be the same again.

A stipulation in his father's will forces Mark back into the arms of a family that disowned him and leaves him one-third owner of a hockey team facing financial ruin. He doesn't even watch hockey, let alone like it, and wants nothing more than to head back to New York. Then there's the new coach, a stubborn, opinionated, irritating man with superiority issues and questionable music taste. Butting heads with Rowen becomes the new normal, but it comes with passionate debate and an all-consuming lust.

Challenged to rebuild one of the worst teams in the league into a future cup contender, Rowen can't pass up the opportunity. Never in his twenty years of hockey has he ever seen a team managed so badly or coached players overflowing with resentment and bigotry. Yet there's something about this team and this city that compels him to roll up his sleeves and start dismantling. If only Mark, one of three siblings who now own the Raptors, wasn't so damned rock-headed yet so damned appealing his job might be easier. It doesn't look like either is willing to give in, but one night in a dark, desert hotel changes everything.

Coast To Coast

Arizona Raptors (Hockey Romance)

1. Coast To Coast
2. Across the Pond
3. Shadow and Light
4. Sugar and Ice
5. School and Rock

Boston Rebels

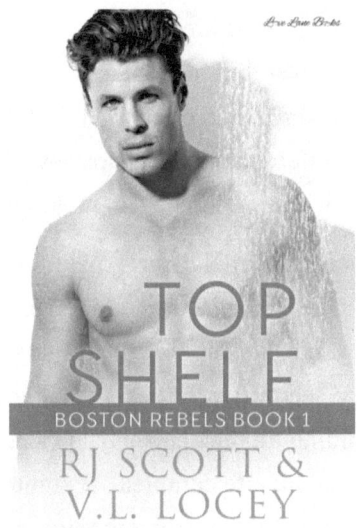

Top Shelf (Boston Rebels 1)

Acting on the attraction to his best friend's brother has always been off the table for Xander until a passionate hookup with Mason at a beach resort begins a love affair that burns long after summer ends.

Mason specializes in assisting same-sex couples on their journey to becoming parents and fighting every rule that blocks his way in the stuck-in-the-past agency that hired him. Living in his brother's pool house is rent-free, and every cent he earns he saves for his dream—that one day he'd have his own company helping others. The downside is that he has to see his annoying brother every day, the upside is that his brother's teammates from the Boston Rebels make regular visits. The eye candy that passes Mason's window is almost enough to make him consider dating a hockey player, but not just any player though. Ever since Xander—his brother's childhood friend—came out as gay at a press conference, Mason's puppy love has turned into a burning attraction he can no longer ignore.

Hockey has been one of Xander's main focuses since he was old enough to balance on skates. Well, hockey and Mason Kingsley, but Mason was always unattainable. Now that he's about to see thirty candles on his birthday cake and is no longer hiding the fact he's gay, he's ready to find a soul mate to make his life complete. A summer vacation is just what he needs to have time to think, but when the Boston Rebels arriving in paradise with Mason in tow, thinking is the last thing he needs. One torrid night under a balmy moon and rules about not messing with his best friend's brother vanish on a warm, tropical breeze.

Summer romances don't generally last past Labor Day, but with the new season about to begin Xander and Mason are going to have to face the world and decide if their love is real enough to withstand everything.

Boston Rebels

Lost In Boston (Free Prequel Novella)

1. Top Shelf
2. Back Check
3. Snowed
4. Royal Lines
5. Blade
6. Rental

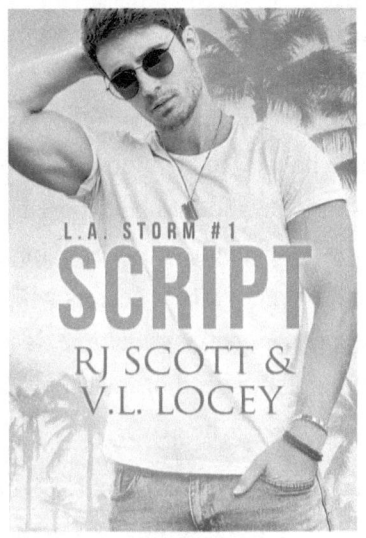

Script (LA Storm, 1)

Script

Hollywood A-lister Finn might be Canadian, but he needs Cameron to show him how to hockey.

Actor Finn Kerrigan is at a crossroads. After growing up a soap star, then starring in a hugely successful trilogy of action movies, he's finally given the chance to read a heartfelt and passionate script that could change his life forever. The role would be enough for people to see him as a serious actor, and maybe even win him an award or two (and no, a golden raspberry award for his action movies doesn't count). Once established as a serious actor he's sure he can come out of the closet and finally live his truth.

When he lies to get the part of a hockey player on a struggling team, he suddenly has nowhere to hide. He might be Canadian, but the last time he skated he was ten, and no, he doesn't have hockey in his blood. With only a month until filming starts, he about to be exposed, but partnered with a player who's supposed to be giving him tips, he doesn't realize how many of his secrets will come to light. Falling in lust, one heated kiss at a time, is inevitable, but giving Cameron up at the end of the shoot could break his heart.

Cameron Chavkin is the face of the LA Storm. And the body, and the hair, and the smile. He's at the prime of his career, men and women want to be with him, and he's skating better than he ever has before. His house sits next to a famous rock star's mansion, his garage is filled with expensive cars, and he's even been asked to mentor a once-famous actor in a new hockey movie. Life is pretty sweet. Until the bad boy of hockey meets Finn, a man on the edge with more secrets than Cameron has endorsements. Knowing better than to get involved, Cameron is swept up despite himself, and when it's time to say goodbye to the Storm's most eligible bachelor is finding it hard to follow the script.

Script

LA Storm

1. Script
2. Second
3. Shield
4. Spiral

Speed (Railers Legacy 1)

Hard ice. Fast cars. Fierce love.

And a race against fate.

Hockey is as natural as breathing for Noah. Growing up with two famous hockey stars as his dads, Noah has always aspired to join the Railers to continue the Lyamin-Gunnarsson legacy. With his degree done, it's time to live that dream, and the first step is being drafted by the team his hall-of-fame dad played for. The second step is to pull on that dusky blue-gray sweater and make his fathers proud. His rookie year is bound to be a season of incredible highs and lows, but one of the biggest highlights is meeting Brody Vance at a fundraiser. Brody is the living epitome of a bad boy hiding his pain behind a devil-may-care attitude. As Noah struggles to keep one eye on the puck and not on Brody, it's only a matter of time before both loves collide in a chaotic splash of media attention.

Bad boy racing driver Brody has spent his life chasing speed and glory and is only points away from his first world championship when a devastating crash ends his season. Determined to make a triumphant comeback, Brody is blindsided by a diagnosis that forces him off the track for good. With his world flipped upside down and family and fans questioning why he left, Brody hides his pain by pushing the limits and refusing to let anyone see the cracks. But after a chance meeting with a sweet, sexy hockey player turns into an unforgettable one-night stand, fate keeps putting Noah in his path. With his heart on the line and his body racing against time, Brody must decide if he's willing to risk it all for love—or if he'll let fear and pride leave him in the dust.

Speed is a steamy M/M romance with a hockey rookie living his family legacy, a bad-boy racing driver with secrets, media attention that would break even the strongest of men, an unforgettable one-night stand, a love that means risking it all, and a hard-won happily ever after.

Railers Legacy

1. *Speed*
2. *Blitz*
3. *Powder*
4. *Fly*

Off The Ice (Chesterford Coyotes, 1)

Off The Ice

**A coming-of-age love story with high school, hockey
rivalry, friendship, family, and coming out.**

Soren's life changes in an instant when he and his younger
brother are adopted by hockey royalty. Making sense of his
new life is hard enough, but when he's enrolled in a private
school it means facing a whole new set of problems.

Navigating friendship, family, and hockey is one thing, but being attracted to the boy who vexes him is a whole new thing.

Felix has a reputation to protect. He's the kid who seems to have everything but looks can be deceiving. Spinning lies about his perfect life, he's created a fantasy world that even he has started to believe. Only, it's not long before everything crumbles, all of his pretty lies are revealed, and only his closest rival sees through his pain and stands by him.

Fighting is easy, friendship is hard, but love is everything.

Off The Ice

Chesterford Coyotes

Free Reads

Please note - in all of these free stories, there will be some spoilers for the main series books.

Railers Short Stories

Volume 1 | Volume 2

LA Storm

Sparkle

The Colts - AHL Short Stories

Pucks & Percentages

Breakaway

Making the Save

Standalone

Waiting for Christmas

Meet RJ Scott

RJ writes MM romance—sometimes sweet, sometimes dark, always with a generous splash of angst and a hint of hurt/comfort.

A born romantic, she's convinced love is love—and every man deserves his happily ever after (especially the ones who swear they don't).

Website - gayromance.co.uk
Newsletter - gayromance.co.uk/mailing-list

instagram.com/rjscott_author
amazon.com/author/rj-scott
bookbub.com/authors/rj-scott

Meet V.L. Locey

V.L. Locey loves worn jeans, yoga, belly laughs, walking, reading and writing lusty tales, Greek mythology, the New York Rangers, comic books, and coffee. (Not necessarily in that order.)

She shares her life with her husband, her daughter, one dog, two cats, a flock of assorted domestic fowl, and two Jersey steers.

When not writing spicy romances, she enjoys spending her day with her menagerie in the rolling hills of Pennsylvania with a cup of fresh java in hand.

vllocey.com | vicki@vllocey.com
Newsletter - vllocey.com/newsletter

facebook.com/V.L.Locey
x.com/vllocey
instagram.com/vl_locey
bookbub.com/authors/v-l-locey
goodreads.com/vllocey
pinterest.com/vllocey